A Life That
You Knew...

...your life, your story

I0666880

A Life That You Knew...

...your life, your story

Saptarshi Basu

Srishti
PUBLISHERS & DISTRIBUTORS

Srishti Publishers & Distributors
N-16, C. R. Park
New Delhi 110 019
srishtipublishers@gmail.com

First published by Srishti Publishers & Distributors in 2013
Copyright © Saptarshi Basu, 2013

All the characters and incidences described in this book are a work of pure
fiction. Any resemblance to any person dead or alive is purely coincidental.

Typeset in AGaramond 12pt. by Suresh Kumar Sharma at Srishti

Acknowledgement

I have always believed that life offers some of the richest sources to draw one's stories from. There is something extra-ordinary about our ordinary lives that merits a tale. As such, that is what I have attempted to do through this book.

This is a fair mix of fact and fiction, of places and people that I, and millions others like me, have come across in our lives. Thus, it would be inappropriate for me to not express my heart-felt gratitude to my family, friends and acquaintances who make this story lively and personal. Finally, it would be ungrateful to not acknowledge Shourya's cherubic smile and Ramni's unflinching support that made this book possible.

1
TIME AND PLACE

India is a vast country. Seventh largest in the world, some of its far-flung areas are separated by as much as six hours of flight. That's about as far as London to Moscow or New York to Texas. When one tries to comprehend India, not only its size, but also its bewildering complexity tends to numb the mind. For, it is a country that has seen uninterrupted habitation for the last 5000 years, or maybe even longer. When man first ventured out of Africa, India lay at the crossroads of this global super-highway of migration. Through the ages as man moved from one corner of the world to the other, he probably paused here for succor and relief, before resuming his epic journey of circumnavigation. Thus, it is India alone that rivals Africa in the diversity of her genes.

Throughout history, people from different races, cultures, religions and regions of the world have crisscrossed the Indian sub-continent and left behind their influence on the collective psyche of the Indian people. While the indigenous Indus Valley Civilization left behind a legacy of complex, urban culture, the Aryan nomads introduced philosophy and abstract thought through their *Vedas*. While the missionary zeal of Ashoka the Great took the teachings of the Buddha to far-off places the Arabs, Turks and Afghans brought Islam to India.

Indeed, modern India is a chaos of different cultures, religions and languages in various stages of indigenization and assimilation. Thus, while the aquiline nose is common in the north-west, high cheekbones are usual in the north east. While the north speaks a multitude of languages derived from Sanskrit, the south converses primarily in one or the other of the four major surviving *Dravidian* languages – a family of languages which people of the Indus Valley Civilization, and maybe all of India, once spoke.

However, nothing in India is quite as it seems to be. To an outsider, these apparent differences of the face and the tongue might seem at odds with one another, but scratch the surface and the differences begin to muddle everything. Centuries of living together has had its toll, and today, there is hardly any among us who has not been influenced by his neighbour. For example, the Bengalis probably share a common lineage with pre-Aryan and Mongoloid people whereas Kannada, a Dravidian language, has an uncanny phonetic resemblance to Sanskrit. While Shiva, probably the most important God in the Hindu Trinity, is inspired by Pashupati of the Indus Valley, the Indian version of Islam is hardly as puritanical as the Arab kind.

So, we are different – but we are quite like one another. What is undeniable though, is the fact that this unique experimentation of inter-mixing has enriched all of us. It has left behind a legacy that is neither this, nor that and is yet fertile with possibilities.

This is the India that never ceases to amaze me, and this is the India that I was born in. There was of course another lesson of a unique Indian nature that I was born with – "Adjust and Accommodate". After all, for nine months, I had to share my mother's womb with my twin sister.

Compared to what my life was destined to become, I had quite an eventful birth. Some men are born with a golden arm – I was born with a broken one. This, the doctors did not realize immediately, but only after a few days. In the meanwhile, so my mother says, I would keep wailing incessantly while she had to confront the usual peskiness.

"Why does he cry so much?"

"Why are his arms always folded?"

"Is it a congenital defect?"

Fortunately for us, the doctors soon diagnosed the reason of my discomfiture and bandaged me up. Incidentally, that stopped the wailing as well – though momentarily.

So, there I was – a five day old baby with an arm in a cast. Sometimes I wonder what I would have felt if I had seen myself like that – pity, indignation, vengeful? Or would I have been what I mostly am these days – simply impassive? Once when I was a young kid, my father happened to show me a gentleman and casually remarked, "Here goes the man who broke your arm." I remember looking at him and feeling nothing. On hindsight, I think I should thank that doctor for gifting me a birth that was somewhat less than commonplace.

Contrary to my infant world of charming innocence, those were turbulent times indeed. Man had landed on the Moon and the west had come up trumps in the space race. The Vietnam War was finally over and the Hippie movement had lost much of its steam. The Watergate scandal had shown the world that even a US president could have feet of clay – it also showed us what free speech could do for a democracy. There were also a couple of other incidents which, unknown to us, had already set in motion developments which were to haunt us for years to come. And they happened right in our backyard – Pakistan and Afghanistan.

It was also a time of great change for India. It was a time for us to reflect and re-invent ourselves. For the first time, we had a generation of youth which had lived in and breathed only free air. Independent for more than thirty years, it was only now that she mustered the courage to take bold steps. Gone were the days of non-aligned and non-committal diplomacy, and she was just beginning to view world events from the practical stand of realpolitik and not from the lofty pedestal of idealism. The success of the Bangladesh War had emboldened the masses and the ignominy of the Sino-Indian War was but a distant past. Albeit brief, it was certainly an age when confidence was in the air.

However, this euphoria was short-lived, and soon the dark clouds of Emergency left no doubts in our mind about what we should not be, but something that we could very easily become. Democracy, in itself, had become an endangered species not only in India, but also in her tempestuous neighbour, Pakistan. A few months ago it had been hung by the noose while the world community helplessly looked on.

Such important geo-political changes could not but impact popular imagination. There was a whiff of change everywhere. The new order was fighting to come out of the shadow of the old, and assert itself in its own right. Where Gavaskar's on-field exploits were just beginning to challenge notions of Indian docility, commercial Hindi cinema of the times was probably, best essaying this ongoing tussle between the old and the new. The 'angry young man', who fought for the underdog and triumphed over the Goliath of the corrupt system, had caught the public fancy. In one go, the world of make-believe romanticism had lost much of its sheen, with some of its biggest proponents fighting a losing battle to hold their own.

Yes. Those were exciting times. But, what would I know? While history was being written, and re-written, I was happily sucking away my thumb to glory!

2
THE FAMILY

I was born in a middle-class, Bengali family – very middle-class, very Bengali. We were *Bangals* – the 'other' Bengalis. At the time of Partition, our ancestors, like a lot of other refugees, crossed over the border into India with only a few personal belongings and a lot of disdain for the *Ghotis* – the Bengalis this side of the border. Uprooted from the land they had been living on for generations and sent packing into the unknown, they sought solace in one another and tended to look down upon habits and practices which they could not fathom. The *Ghoti* and his customs were, for us, bastardized forms of the real thing. This implied that *Bangal-Ghoti* alliances were unholy, that "East-Bengal" was the only football club worth following and that the love of *Ilish*, the Tenualosa Ilisha, was much more refined than the liking for *Chingri*, the king prawn.

Incidentally, close to three decades after Partition when my father got married, the match was with a girl from a similar immigrant background. Care was further taken to ensure that she came from a village close by to his original village in Dhaka.

Of course, as I later realized, most of the assumed superiority was hogwash – a desperate attempt by a dispossessed people to cling on to their roots, in the face of tremendous adversity. To compound this urge for self-preservation, there was the inevitable scarcity of resources that pitted immigrants against locals. Though Hindu-Muslim unity was the obvious casualty of Partition, the tensions between the dispossessed and the settled were by no means less significant. With the passage of time, however, the schisms of the latter variety proved to be much less intransigent than the former.

That my grandfather came from Dhaka I am sure of, but the fact that he chose Jalpaiguri at the foot of the Himalayas, over much closer places to the east, is somewhat intriguing. For, if one looks at the map, the road from Dhaka to Jalpaiguri runs through miles of the erstwhile East Pakistani territory. The choice looks unlikely, probably a touch irrational and, in the absence of hard evidence, conjecture can be my only recourse.

It would be important, however, to keep in mind that in the run up to the Partition, there was a fair bit of confusion about the delineation of borders between India and Pakistan, with the fate of individual towns, cities and districts being open to speculation. Adding to the general chaos was the terrible bloodshed unleashed by communal strife. Did my grandfather choose this, a much longer route, to avoid the wave of refugees coming in from the east? Did he, the son of a farmer, find the rain-fed and mineral-rich lands of Jalpaiguri much more preferable than the urban dwelling of Calcutta? Had one of his kin already settled in Jalpaiguri before the Partition, making it less alien? Or, had he in a fit of panic, hastily grabbed a few personal possessions and taken the first road away from the trauma?

I would never know for sure, but what was telling was that he eventually decided to settle down at a place in India which was tantalizingly close to the border.

If my grandfather had the benefit of hindsight, he would have taken heart from the fact that the journey from Dhaka to India, though full of trials and tribulations, was like a speck of dust on the sands of time. Some years ago, I had got my gene sample mapped as part of a global study on the migration of the human race. What I learnt about the journey that my primordial ancestors undertook simply dwarfed and humbled my imagination. The story starts 50,000 years ago, in the Rift Valley of north-east Africa. This was when my earliest ancestor lived and his was the only lineage that survived outside Africa, making him the common ancestor of every non-African living today. Probably driven by scarcity or by curiosity, this scientific Adam made the first great journey to the unknown. As aeons passed, this gentleman and his descendents traversed an epic route through the Middle East, Central Asia, the Pamir Knot and then north onto southern Siberia before finally turning back and ending up in the Indian sub-continent. They faced tremendous hardships and near annihilation along the way – but their resilience and survival instincts saw them overcome all odds and proliferate in different parts of the world.

When I look at it, fights over race, region and religion seem so pointless. Such large spans of time and distance could hardly have been covered without a thought or two for the fellow beside. I think that differences have their own place in society, but the instinct to collaborate and thrive is much more ancient – much more basic.

As an infant, I was quite a handful. Today, I am ill-at-ease among strangers – I was even less sociable as a kid. Well, frankly speaking, I was obnoxious. Babies cry to seek attention – I cried for the heck of it. I would cry if I was hungry, I would cry if I was over-fed. I would cry if I was sleepy, I would cry if I was not feeling sleepy. But, I would mostly cry if Mom was not around. So much so, that a decent shower became somewhat of a luxury for her. As she rushed through her daily ablutions, I would be outside the shower-room clasping the end of her *sari* that she would, thoughtfully but unsuccessfully, hang out to comfort me. Oh, did I also tell you that my high-decibel exertions would leave my sister terrified out of her wits?

I was a difficult baby – but my Mom, too, was the Amazon incarnate.

My elder brother was quite young, about six, when my sister and I were born. Mom had a difficult time managing the two new-borns and, with little help forthcoming, she had to take some time away from her eldest kid. In a sense, my brother grew up when he was six and Mom would nurse this guilt throughout her life. One day, when we were a few months old, my little elder brother was arranging the bed for the two of us to sleep on. Seeing this and unable to hold back the flood of emotions that overwhelmed her, she burst into tears.

That was how my brother had to rush through his tender years – but that was not all. Unknown to us, the cruel hand of fate would need him to toughen up once again.

A close-knit family, we lived an ordinary but a reasonably comfortable life. Though not stuffed with toys and the like, we did have everything to set ourselves up for the future. We ate well, went to the best schools, had good books to read and were blessed to have an environment conducive to learning. On the other hand, we seldom laid our hands on a gaming console or went to exotic vacations. Like all other Dads, ours too wanted to do the best for us, and the best he did. My father could not leave us a big inheritance, but he taught us a few handy things. He built us in his own image and had a unique way of making things simple. He would often say,

"We were a lot of kids and my father could not give us much time. If we had not worked hard, we would have been rotting today…"

Needless to say, we grew up on a healthy diet of "make an honest effort, make your own destiny". I am not really sure if I have been able to take control of my life, but I think I have been largely sincere in what I have done. Ultimately, this was the singularly most important gift that we got from Dad.

⌒

I don't remember much from my toddler days, but the memory of a hot, summer afternoon sticks out particularly well. I remember sitting on my grandfather's lap looking straight ahead out of the window. The window of my grandfather's house overlooked a cemented path, running through a garden and leading on to the main-gate. The pathway was bordered on either side by rows of bougainvillea, roses and palm trees. It was a big house with lots of mysterious, dark corners and poisonous snakes.

I can still see that sunny afternoon as if it were yesterday. It must have been around two, and I was feeling a little drowsy from the rice at lunch. There was not a sound to be heard, save the occasional crow or myna. It was as if the heat had lulled everything around me into a deep slumber. I was, however, quite comfortable with the dazzling brightness of the sun outside only serving to accentuate the cool darkness inside. Through the bars of the open window, I could see a postman laboriously cycling towards our house, while my grandpa kept gently humouring me in the background with childish prattle.

This rather insignificant memory has remained with me as some kind of a defining image of childhood. Even today, in a lazy afternoon, I am transported to that hot, *Terai* summer. On days such as these, I lie on my bed and stare blankly at the whitewashed ceiling. I can vividly see the postman cycling towards me – except that there is no grandpa humming in the background and no birds in the concrete monstrosity that I call home.

Grandpa, a farmer at heart and a policeman by profession, was a man of contradictions. Always the one for hospitality, he could be quite brusque with his guests. Once he had thrown an elaborate party, lavish by any stretch of imagination. Cutlets and fish-fries to start with, a main course of *pulao, chholar daal, kosha mangsho, chitol-er muttha, illish bhape* that finally ended with *papad, chutney, doi, roshogolla, sandesh* and *pan.* He had gone much beyond his means and that made him happy. As he surveyed the guests relishing every bit of the delicious food that he had so painstakingly arranged, he had a self-contented smile on his face.

Then, somebody came up and remarked – "*Chitto babu*, the cutlets are great!"

Pat came the reply – "There's none left!"

Yes, he could be tough. As a career policeman, he had spent the better part of his life disciplining thugs and criminals. That strict sense of discipline extended to other facets of his life as well. With a strapping physique and an acerbic tongue, he loved to intimidate. I was too young to remember much of this, but I know that he could be dreadful in a rage. He had many beliefs, and his beliefs were sacrosanct. He believed that a son's duty to his parents was supreme and that filial obligations should always take precedence over marital ones. He expected blind devotion from his sons and mute obedience from their wives, and giving so much as an understanding ear to the spouse in matters of household dispute was tantamount to betrayal. In his mind, the man, the woman and the children of the house had very fixed and rigid roles to perform – the man would buy the fish and the woman would cook it. The children would work hard, grow up and provide for the parents in their old age. And thus, the wheel of dharma would keep spinning.

With the benefit of hindsight, I am now quite ambivalent towards the way that grandpa thought about life. He lived in an age of scarcity. Managing a household of eight, with meager resources, was by no means an easy task. Scarcity enforced strict rules and demanded unquestioned obedience from the family members. Unity was strength, and observance of rules was the glue which held families together. Whatever little that a honest, hard-working policeman made those days, was barely enough to provide for the basic needs of life. Thus, the children, if they wanted to do anything with their lives, had to necessarily be sincere and self-reliant – there was nobody to give them a leg-up in life. If nothing else, then the value of an honest effort and the pride of self-achievement were the most significant legacies that our elders bequeathed on us.

Where my grandpa, and numerous other men like him, missed out was in not becoming more flexible to the demands of changing times. Though the strict patriarchal hierarchy could bind families together, it could also breed a stifling environment. The freedom to think and act differently had no place in a regimented world as this. Not giving an equal say to the women of the house was downright unfair that would eventually have sowed seeds of sedition. Grandpa was fortunate in having a dutiful son, an obedient daughter-in-law and not a joint family in the strictest sense, but there must have been hundreds of others, not as fortunate. That would inevitably have led to a lot of tension and eventual break-up of families.

Today, the institution of joint family is on life support. But, for all its imperfections, it did sustain a generation of Indians. It provided an able framework for emotional nourishment. Its greatness lay in the fact that it could teach an individual to put others before the self. These days, most of us live in nuclear families and the bonds that tie parents to their children and siblings to one another, the bonds that are so uniquely Indian, are getting increasingly tenuous.

The last time I went home, for a couple of weeks, was almost a year back. Whenever I think about the people that were once an indispensable part of my daily life and whom I get to see so rarely these days, it makes me feel hollow. The mother who bore you in her womb, the father who taught you to walk, the brothers and sisters that shared your moments of joy and sorrow, how little of them do you see today! When was the last time you had a meal together – when was the last time you shared a joke? Some are old, some are long gone while some are far, far away. Rushing from one meeting to another, worrying about the next deadline, we hardly spare a moment for those wonderful memories of childhood. Maybe that's what passage of time is meant to be, but it still leaves an emptiness that is very hard to fill.

3
THE WHITE ELEPHANTS

*D*urgapur is a dusty, provincial town, off the arterial Grand Trunk Road, about 150 kilometers from Calcutta. The Grand Trunk Road, known variously as *Uttarapatha, Badshahi Sadak* or N.H. – 2 (depending on what point in time you are talking about) occupies a pretty important place in Indian history. Running roughly parallel to the Ganga, it has always been a strategic link between the east and the west. Apparently initiated in the 3rd century BC by the Mauryan empire, it was later renovated and extended by Sher Shah Suri. Originally built as a trade transit, it emerged as the administerial backbone of the empires of Sher Shah, the Mughals and the British. Close to 2,500 kilometers, it runs from Sonargaon through Dhaka in the east to Kabul in the west. Along the way fall some of the greatest historical sites – places like Sasaram, Varanasi,

Allahabad, Agra, Delhi, Panipat, Amritsar, Lahore, Peshawar, the Khyber Pass and Jalalabad.

Indeed, the GT Road is steeped in history and my pulse starts racing, each time I travel by it. I wonder how great it would be if I could drive down the GT Road to Kabul and go back in time. Will I come across the Gandhara princes on their way to the battle of Kurukshetra? Will I find Alexander, exhausted from his many wars slouching in the shade of a banyan tree? Will I come across a young Babur on his course to making history? Will I see Shah Jahan, on a moonlit night, gazing wistfully at his labour of love? Or will I bump across Netaji, eager with his dreams of a free India and barely suppressing a childlike excitement at being able to hoodwink the mighty British, as he drove at a breakneck pace through the dead of night? Oh! If only I had a time machine!

The GT road is ancient, but Durgapur has no such pretensions. It is a nondescript, industrial town with a recorded history going back no further than half a century. In its present shape, it is the product of a naïve era of Nehruvian socialism when state-sponsored large industries were thought to be the vehicles which could fast forward India on the path to growth and development. In its heyday, Durgapur was the prodigal child of Dr. B.C. Roy. It had some of the biggest names in industry including the Steel Authority of India Ltd., the Heavy Engineering Corpn., Hindustan Fertilizer, the Eastern

Coalfields Ltd. and numerous others. It counted distinguished guests as visitors – Pt. Jawaharlal Nehru, Dr. Rajendra Prasad and even Queen Elizabeth! Endowed with rich mineral resources and great geographical advantage, it seemed it could do no wrong.

And then came the fall. After the initial days of romance were over, the PSUs, as they were called, could not achieve the desired rate of productivity and began to flounder on the much touted promises. It became evident that too much money was going into them and not much was coming out. Over a period of time, they became such a huge burden on the exchequer that they were dubbed as "the white elephants". About the same time, the Left Front unseated the Congress Government (and reigned for a good 34 years!) in the state of West Bengal, and fell out of favour with the government at the centre. The prodigal child was presently orphaned, and the industry decimating policies of the Left sounded a death-knell for the "Ruhr of the East".

When I was born, Durgapur was already living on borrowed time. Once as a young boy, I had asked my father –

"Will your factory close down?"

He had said, "Don't worry son. I have been hearing that ever since I joined it. Nothing's going to happen!"

That Durgapur, and the likes of it, were places of stagnation, a relic of the past that India had chosen to forget, hardly ever bothered me. What I found more irksome was that there were no legends about the city of my birth. It was a constant irritant till one day I came across *Bhabani Pathak-er Tila*.

The *Tila* was actually the ruins of an old watchtower. Strategically situated on a mound overlooking the GT Road, it had winding stone steps leading up to the base of a tower of burnt bricks – though not much of a tower as the rump of one. The roof had caved in, and in its place was a dark, gaping hole that went deep inside the ground for as far as the eye could see. Legend has it, that it was built by *Bhabani Pathak* – a local chieftain, more than a hundred and fifty years ago, when Durgapur was still wild, unmapped territory.

It was not much, but still old enough for my youthful imagination. I would dream about those secretive tunnels that apparently ran from the base of the tower to the river Damodar. What mystery were they hiding? Did *Bhabani Pathak* use them to smuggle men and materials away from the prying eyes of the emperor? Why had he built the tower? Who was he afraid of and who did he want to keep an eye on? Was it to plunder hapless travelers on the GT Road? I neither tried nor received any concrete answers to these questions. Maybe I was afraid that the truth would be far less fantastic and thus I remained contented by letting my imagination run riot.

Till some years ago, the ruins of the old watch tower used to dominate the horizon and seeing the tired evening sun go down on it was quite a spectacle. The sun would keep marching onto the ruins, almost inexorably as if pulled by some irresistibly fatal attraction. For a while it would hover impatiently, rendering the burnt brick of the tower a desolate, unearthly orange. And then, with a last flourish, it would vanish abruptly as if gobbled up by the hungry, open mouth of the old watchtower.

It was a sight that would thrill me and I wondered that in a land as ancient as India, can one really find a place that does not have a legend!

Thirty years ago, Durgapur had a very different profile. Contrary to cities which grow spontaneously, it did not have much of a defining character. It is true that there is a geographic and economic reason behind the coming up of any human habitat, but where such habitat is allowed to grow unhurriedly; it evolves over a period time to develop a personality of its own. It is a personality that has, in due course of time, absorbed and assimilated the different undercurrents within itself and given rise to a culture that is very personal and very unique. It is a culture that is living and vibrant and finds expression through its inhabitants.

Durgapur was different. It was a human endeavour that hadn't had time to come into its own. It was the masterplan of an architect unceremoniously imposed on an alien landscape. It had the basic framework, but was yet to develop the flesh and the sinew which could make it a living, throbbing city. It was still a city of discrete parts that had contiguous borders, but had yet to evolve a unity of expression.

Each of these parts had their own nucleus and was essentially a self-contained unit. We called these 'colonies' or 'townships'. The bigger of the several companies in Durgapur had townships of their own – while the smaller ones just piled on. A township had houses for the employees, schools for the kids, hospitals for the sick, clubs and cinemas for recreation, shopping plazas and other infrastructure necessary for the conduct of everyday life. What a township also had was a character of its own and often, quite different from the one just beside it. Usually, a township assumed the character of its people, who in turn tended to be overtly influenced by the state of affairs of the company they worked for. Thus, there were townships which were very cosmopolitan and townships which were very provincial. Some appeared progressive and youthful and others were incorrigibly morose. While some looked towards the future with eager anticipation, others looked back with a hint of pensiveness.

Amidst this sea of contradictions, there was one unifying theme that came closest to being the 'character of Durgapur'. Beyond all these differences, we were basically a group of people from the hinterlands of India, moulded into the orderly structure of a 'planned' economy. Like the 'sameness' of our surroundings, there was a 'sameness' in our thinking and our dreams. We wanted to be doctors or engineers and were embarrassingly uncomfortable in the presence of the opposite sex. Our provincial background stressed on the content rather than the form. Truth be told, we were earthy – we lacked panache!

I lived in a box shaped building, in one such 'colony'. The building had four apartments spread over two floors. Ours was one of the ground floor flats. There were three decent-sized living rooms, a spacious kitchen and a cramped shower arranged along the sides of a rectangular verandah. Two doors led to the garden which surrounded the house. The garden was quite bare – we had a few lilies, some ornamental shrubs, a lone cactus, the humble *tagar*, the ubiquitous *sal* and a decaying guava tree. The garden, as well as the house, was unapologetically utilitarian. There wasn't an iota of ornamentation, rather a somberness that was all-pervasive.

But I loved it. I had been in that house for as long as I could remember, and had, in time, developed a strong sense of kinship. Every inch was familiar and you could barely move around without brushing past one cherished memory or the other. The wall I scribbled on, the edge of the table that gave me the scar on my forehead, the tree that seduced me with its juicy fruits, the window through which I gazed out aimlessly, the corner where I vented my adolescent rage, the bed I dreamt on, the cabinet I hung my clothes in, the mirror which I spoke to at length, the smell of the first monsoon shower – were all bits of me that had remained frozen in time. For a better part of my life, that was home.

⌒

Colony life was simple and uncomplicated. Your social trappings were determined by your designation. Your designation, in turn, was determined by the number of years you had put in. When you joined the organization, you were put in a bachelor accommodation. As you progressed, you moved into bigger houses, bigger rooms, bigger gardens and increasingly smaller social circles. Our colony had different types of apartments – starting from the very humble bachelor quarters to the expansive bungalows for the top executives. While the bachelors' apartments were marked by the camaraderie of communal living, the top-end houses were distinguished by window mounted air-conditioners and car parks. Huge and rusty, the air-conditioners had little time for aesthetics or mechanical efficiency. Durgapur was a small town without many places to go to and thus, like the air-conditioners, cars too were more of a status symbol. Car-owners were few and cars to choose from were even fewer. Though dilapidated "second-hand" Ambassadors were clearly more preferred, some were bold enough to opt for the gleaming, new Maruti 800s. Yes, the Maruti 800 was quite a phenomenon. It was small, dandy and had an engine that was like a faithful Indian wife – it would ignite without tantrums and run without as much as a whimper. In the drab world of the Ambassadors and Premier Padminis, it was, clearly, a much refreshing change.

For the hoi-polloi, on the other hand, bikes were still the preferred mode of transportation. Unassuming and sturdy they, in taking our Dads to their offices or entire families on outings, were faithful companions which took us places.

Our fathers must have had dreadfully boring professional lives. They would start at the stroke of 7 and finish by 4 in the evening. At about 11 in the morning, they would come home for lunch. I would often be curious about what is it that they did at work. I would ask my Dad –

"You keep saying that your company is always short of orders. What, then, do you work on?" Somewhat evasively, he would answer, "There are always some orders to be worked on."

That kind of an answer would never satisfy me, but I hardly ever probed deeper.

It may well be that the government, in its infinite wisdom, had figured out a way to keep people unproductively employed. Did the employees ever worry about the purposefulness of their jobs? As they meandered through a lifetime of frightening hierarchy, I wonder what kept them going!

If there ever were a void in our Dads' professional lives, it was more than made up for by the vibrancy of their social lives. They joined their jobs as dreamy-eyed young men and had streaks of silver, when they were done. With time, colleagues became friends and friends became brothers. Theirs was a genuine bond of love forged through the ups and downs of life. Be it the vows of matrimony, the birth of a child, the spring-time picnic with the kids, the celebration of a child's successes, the passing away of a kin, anniversaries or the simple everyday marital tiffs – they shared every happiness, every sorrow whether small or big. Together, they had built up a superb support system where there were all for one and one for all. And, as for us kids, neighbours were the only extended family we knew.

That we were all of more or less the same age helped a lot. We went to the same schools, played the same games and liked to do the same things. While there were several aspects of our colony life that I loved, I looked forward most eagerly to the birthday parties. Those were one of the rare occasions when we could take a break from the rigidity of discipline. Long before the advent of satellite television and in a sleepy town like Durgapur, we did not have much by way of entertainment. However, even parents would make an exception for birthdays. Birthdays meant sumptuous dinners. Birthdays meant the twin delights of hogging with the guests and then opening gift wraps once they were gone. Weird as it might sound, we seldom cut cakes or decorated our houses with balloons – we probably felt that it was too pansy!

By far, the most awaited event of our birthday parties was the movie screening at the end. For that, we would specially hire "video cassette players" from the neighbourhood parlour. The video cassette player, or VCP as we would call it, was an amazing contraption from a bygone era of analog circuits when big was beautiful. Huge and boxy, it had a neat horizontal slit in the front for the cassette to go in. One had to only guide the cassette slightly towards the slit and the VCP would lustily grab it in like a lover pining for the beloved. This conjugal bliss would result in three hours of wholesome entertainment for us. The video would be grainy; the device might decide to malfunction at the most climactic moments leading to a frenetic activity to bang it into life – but we didn't seem to mind. *Born Free, ET, Ram Lakhan* or *Shahenshah*, this was how we got introduced to the thrill of cinema. It was the thrill of being transported to a dream world where everything was possible. It was the thrill of eagerly waiting for the denouement through the battery of interruptions. It was a thrill which has probably been dulled in recent times by the surfeit of movie-viewing options available.

Durgapur had a tropical climate with hot summers, wet monsoons and a fleetingly cold winter. It was dotted with *sal* trees – remnants of the once impenetrable deciduous forest that used to abound in the region. The vegetation would give each season a unique colour. During spring, the trees would shed their leaves and the earth would be covered by a thick carpet of gold while a velvet of green would spring up with the first monsoon shower.

Summer was, however, an entirely different matter. Scalding and unrelenting in its heat, it would stretch on for five long months – from March to July. The Sun would be up pretty early and by noon it would get incredibly hot. Afternoons would be desolate affairs with every living being desperately looking for much needed respite under elusive shades. Those who dared to venture out would have their faces wrapped with pieces of wet cotton as protection against the scorching *loo* blowing in from the west. With eyes peering from behind the white cover, they would look like zombies inhabiting a wasted land. Save these few brave souls, it would be pretty still otherwise. The heat could be quite tricky as well. At times, as I lazily dozed off, I would hear a shrill, drumming sound coming from some far-off land. Unsure of itself, it would start off tentatively, gradually rise to a crescendo and then cease all of a sudden, as if smothered by an invisible hand. Mom would later explain –

"That's *Takshak,* the King of Snakes, holding his *durbar!*"

Moms! They come up with such fantastically simple explanations for everything!

Those long, lazy afternoons would also be occasions when I would give a shot at interpreting science lessons. And, my half-baked knowledge, would often lead to undesirable results. One day, after reading that water evaporating from a surface can cool down the temperature of the surroundings and that it was a technique used in air coolers, I decided to try it out myself. I dipped a bed-sheet in water and hung it from the window. I also reasoned with myself that, in order to prevent the heat from coming in from outside, I should close down all the windows. I did that and lay in the room, hoping fervently that it would cool down. However, in a short while, the room became so damp and oppressive that I had no option but to unceremoniously discard all scientific pretensions. Science, it seemed to me, had its limits!

It was only later that I realized that I had missed a very critical component that for evaporating water to cool down the surroundings, one needed to ensure free circulation of air; or, in other words, the windows had to be kept open!

Meanwhile, the summer would go on with a seemingly endless

obsession to beat down to submission, everything that came in its way. The trees would go bare, the land would crack up and the Damodar would shrink to an apology of a river, till man and beast alike would yearn for a divine palliative to relieve them of the suffering. A thousand prayers would not go in vain and Nature the bountiful, finally moved by the all-round misery, would pour her heart out.

After all the waiting, the monsoons would not disappoint us – they would be pretty grand. The *Kal Boishakhi* would herald the onset of the rainy season. But even before the *Kal Boishakhi*, the air would smell of rain. Towards the end of months of rampant heat, the air would begin taking a damp odour. The moisture would still keep the days quite warm, but the humidity and the unnatural calmness of late afternoons would tell us that relief was at hand. The heaviness of the wet air would suggest that the heavens were dying to burst open any moment. Before long, dark, ominous clouds would amass on the horizon and the *Kal Boishakhi* would come in as a violent, dusty storm purging the earth off the last remains of the summer. The stage would be set for the rains to soothe the bruises of a much-tortured land.

The impact of the first few drops of rain would be quite dramatic. Cool, as they would be – on touching the parched, hot ground they would recoil as jets of steam, like a coy, teenage girl who instinctively withdraws after the initial brushing of lips at her first kiss. Those first few, insufficient drops would make the earth even thirstier, and an irresistibly, sweet scent of longing would beseech the skies for more. Soon, the skies would oblige and come down in a torrential downpour bringing the much needed succour to one and all.

The monsoons would be a time of plenty, and after months of severe penance, Nature would wallow in her own excesses. The dry, dusty earth would become wet and muddy. Puddles of water would form on every available depression and tiny rivulets would run through every available crack. A thick canopy of green would envelop every exposed surface. This sudden generosity would also lead to an explosion in insect life. The vigorous croaking of the frogs and the glow of the fireflies would keep us awake till late at night.

As a kid, the rains would evoke mixed feelings in me. On the one hand, I could not but celebrate this sudden benevolence, while on the other there would be a degree of indignation at being short-changed. That every evening it would rain heavily, thus robbing me of my game of football, would seem like some malicious cosmic conspiracy. As the skies got dark, and brilliant flashes of lightning pierced the thick sheet of rain, I would stand near the window and gaze into the horizon. With the pitter patter of the falling rain in the background punctuated by the rumblings of the occasional thunder, I would get transported to a similar rainy evening at my grandfather's.

I would long for the rhythmic beating of the raindrops falling on sheets of asbestos that made up the roof of my grandfather's place at Jalpaiguri. And, I would nag myself –

"Why does it have to rain in the evenings?" "Why can't it rain in the mornings and give me more 'rainy days'!"

4
LIKE GOLD IN A FURNACE

The 'rainy day' was, of course, a great concept. Whenever it rained heavily, we would get a day off from school. The whole unexpectedness of those holidays was made even sweeter by the fact that, on occasions we would actually discover that the school was closed, only after reaching the premises. Ah! Those were the days – we could afford to have days off and yet not worry about having to come on a Saturday to make up for the lost time. It was fun.

My first introduction to school was pretty intimidating. I remember the day when I went for the admission test. The building was much bigger than my modest pre-school and I think I had asked –

"Is that a hospital, Dad?"

Dad's reply was something like –

"In a way, yes. They both make people better."

I don't remember much of the admission test itself; except that I was given a set of jumbled up building blocks and asked to reproduce the picture of a bird. Sitting on Dad's lap, I had fiddled around with the pieces till the Principal, an elderly-looking Belgian Father, had kindly inquired –

"So, son, what do you think it is?"

To which, I had given the one-word reply – "*Bok!*"

"He means a pelican, *Bok* is the Bengali for pelican" – Dad had helpfully offered.

I am not sure what Father Wavreil was looking for, but I made it.

While pre-school was the place that I initially came into contact with people outside my family, school was the first time that I had ever gone out of home, alone. Sis and I used to go to pre-school together, and she, clearly the tougher between the two, would chaperone me around. Thus, school was where I actually started developing my social skills. It's a process that has continued to this day and yet there is much room for development. It would be fair to say that now I am only slightly more comfortable, socially, than I was at the beginning. Even to this day, I am usually the guy who goes to a party, looks around for familiar faces, makes sheepish attempts at trying to butt into a conversation at inopportune moments, gobbles up the food, then hangs around aimlessly for a while before finally fidgeting into the background. Yes, I am the guy who nobody notices in a crowd.

Mrs. Moore, our kindergarten teacher, was a motherly lady. With a smattering of Bengali, that she spoke, she tried her best to make us feel at home. While introducing us to the rudiments of formal education, she would also give us some of the very first lessons in social etiquette. Even her admonishment had a touch of affection to it. It was, thus, curiously funny how I managed to concoct imaginary fears about her.

It so happened that I had, in a playful mood, been quite extravagant in using the new set of sketch pens on my text book. In order to stop me from dirtying the book further, Mom had casually remarked –

"Wait till your teacher sees this!"

Mom had left it at that, but I took it further. Paranoia hit me hard, and, in my mind I started going through all the different ways that I could be punished for my frivolity. Would I get an old-fashioned thrashing or, worse still, would I be made to stand outside the classroom? I could put up with the physical aspect, but how would I ever deal with the humiliation! As I lay on my bed that night, I racked my brains for all the possible outcomes, but each one looked darker than the other. The future seemed bleak.

By morning, my obsession became so manic that feigning illness seemed the last resort. And so, I was afflicted by a sudden bout of stomach cramps. It was so acute that I lay writhing in agony while the entire world got ready to go to school. The pain was sudden, severe and opportunistic. It would reach its painful climax as the school-bus rolled in and would subside a few minutes after the bus was out of sight.

The morning charade would continue for a few days, before Mom began to suspect that something was amiss. She informed Dad, and together they started wearing down my childish defence. Dad was stern –

"You cannot skip school like this. What is your problem?"

Mom provided the human touch –

"What are you afraid of? Don't worry, we are here."

This went on for a while, and before long, unable to fend off the barrage of questions, I found myself blurting out the truth.

Mom, Dad and, later, Mrs. Moore, went through the ridiculousness of the situation with all the seriousness that it demanded. They talked to me about the enormity of the crime, but added that a 'one-time exception' could be made. Relieved, I vowed never again to violate a rule so blantantly.

Spread over a sprawling campus of fifty acres, my school was a couple of decades old by the time I got in. A dense growth of *sal* trees fenced it, cutting us off from the hustle-bustle of everyday life. If someone were to look down from the sky, our school would have appeared like a little clearing in the midst of a thick forest. That wouldn't have been too far from reality – our school was every bit the oasis that it seemed.

Packed in grey coloured buses, with iron-grills for windows, we would troop in everyday around eight in the morning and leave by one in the afternoon. Thus, we had a five hour day and a five day week. Our Moms were homemakers and schools, those days, had no need to be intense, day-long affairs. For good or bad, school was mostly about studying and extra-curricular activity was a personal choice best left to the interest and discretion of the individual concerned. We were not forced to participate in inter-school debates or sports competitions. But yes, a five-hour day meant that we had ample time to do what we wanted. When we did take part in quiz contests or sports, it was out of genuine interest and not by compulsion.

By the standards of the day and the place, we were a slightly 'elitist' school – though, with monthly tuition fees in the range of a hundred-and-twenty rupees, we paid peanuts compared to what one needs to shell out today. However, it would be naïve to think that a hundred-and-twenty was an easy amount for all our parents. There were definitely a few for whom it was mere change, for most like us it was a decently big sum of money and for certain others it meant a tough choice of foregoing some worldly comforts for the kid's education. I remember a friend of mine whose family had fallen on particularly hard times as his father's factory had shut down. One day, visibly animated, he came and announced –

"Guess what, we sold our TV yesterday. Dad says that we will buy a bigger and better one in a few days!"

I doubt if he got his TV in the promised 'few days'; but, he did go on to finish his studies, and, in due course of time, did get to own a much better TV and a lot of other personal possessions as well.

We came from backgrounds of diverse levels of affluence. What united us was the premium that we put on education. For working class people like us, a solid educational grounding was the only way to move up in life. No wonder we worshipped *Ma Saraswati*, the goddess of learning, with a lot more fanfare than *Ma Lakshmi*, the goddess of wealth.

Our school was an able alibi in this universal respect for education. In the homogeneity of our unassuming, grey-and-white school-uniform, we were able to set aside our differences and accord a degree of dignity to the blood and sweat of our parents who had put us there, sometimes at tremendous cost to themselves. For the most part, we were sincere and did not let their sacrifices go in vain.

In our unity of purpose, we aspired to be like gold in a furnace, as our school-motto so poetically claimed.

⌒

We were affiliated to the I.C.S.E. board, but we went much beyond the prescribed syllabus. Performance in the board exams was an important barometer of success, but we tended to think of it not as an end in itself, but as the natural outcome of a much more comprehensive understanding of different subjects. We knew 'Mathematics' not as a slender I.C.S.E. textbook, but as a complex discipline which had elements of 'Arithmetic', 'Algebra' and 'Geometry'. While 'Science' meant 'Physics', 'Chemistry' and 'Biology', 'Social Science' was 'History', 'Civics' and 'Geography'.

My personal favourite was Geometry. To me, it was a subject that gave you a set of basic tools, theorems or axioms, with which you could deduce patterns in other, much more complex designs. One required very little of learning by rote; instead, creative interpretation and logical reasoning could take you a long way. For precisely the same reasons, I hated Chemistry.

Our school practised a novel form of a 'loyalty scheme' for 'incentivization' in an academic context. We were graded on all the different subjects and the topper of each was given a 'privilege card' that carried a specific number of 'points' with it. One could also get a privilege card for 'good conduct'. We could keep accumulating the privilege cards and at the end of the term, depending on the points accrued, we could redeem it against a set of books. I am not sure whose brainchild this scheme was, but I am pretty sure that *Abhro da* had a hand in choosing the books we read. In a way, it was *Abhro da's* careful selection and thoughtfulness that inculcated the love of books in our young minds.

Abhro da had an immense command over the English language and was a walking encyclopedia of history and current affairs. A brilliant student, he had been a regular contributor to children's magazines and had won many prizes in quiz contests in his time. Tall, wiry with a curved beak of a nose that did a neat job of balancing the horn-rimmed spectacles, he looked every inch an intellectual. Erudite and scholarly, he was destined for much bigger things. So, it must have been quite upsetting, when personal exigencies made him settle for the relative obscurity of teachership in the slightly-known school of an unknown town. In order to overcome the pain of unfulfilled ambitions that had left a bitter after taste in his mouth, he had sought solace and found fulfillment in the world of books. Fiercely introspective by nature, he came across as aloof and arrogant to those who didn't know him well.

Abhro da taught us English and History. However, it was the school-library where his heart lay. He had assumed a voluntary guardianship of the library and devoted most of his after-work hours to it. An avid book lover himself, he knew how to stimulate bibliophilism. He had taken great care to stock the library with some of the rarest works of art. In this, his endeavour was not to overwhelm the prospective reader with an excess of literary abstraction, but to titillate his senses enough so that he got encouraged to explore for himself.

I would look forward to the weekly library visit with a great deal of anticipation and as I entered the cramped quarters, my eyes would light up with greed. They would scan the rows of catalogued books tidily stacked on the shelves and then fall on the new arrivals carelessly strewn on the floor. I would have about an hour in which to quickly go through the summaries at the back and then pick the one I wanted. There was a lot to choose from – Enid Blyton and Robert Louis Stevenson to Tolstoy and Kafka. However, a young romantic, I would more often go in for Corbett.

As a young boy, I had a particular liking for the thrill of the unknown. Probably the predictability of my daily routine made me yearn for a night in the forest. Tiptoeing through the dense blanket of solitude with the stillness pierced at times by the shrillness of the chital, the soft music of the hilly stream of water rushing past the pebbles with the lonely *Kumaon* as a benign guardian, the setting sun that suffused the western horizon with a pale orange, waiting for nightfall in the machaan and, gun-in-hand, keeping a vigil over the lurking shadows of the *Man-eater of Rudraprayag* – seemed to me the ultimate in adventure that one could hope for. Jim Corbett was a man who had lived and worked in the forest. A naturalist and conservationist, his vivid visual imagery would bring the Garhwal to life. As I leafed through the pages, the flora and fauna would beckon me and I would feel a burning desire to go live among them.

Another favourite was Ray's Feluda. Feluda is a super-sleuth who has captured the imagination of generations of Bengalis. To me, Feluda was a slightly watered down Sherlock Holmes but a much more culturally sensitive Indiana Jones. As is the wont of most detectives, he enjoyed using his superior cerebral skills and keen observation powers to unmask the most devious of villains. But, in doing so, he would also give us an insight into the legends of faraway lands. Twenty years ago, the world was a much bigger place and travel was lesser and far in between. It was the exploits of characters like Feluda that filled up this void and became our window to the world. Ray's treatment of Feluda was masterly – he had an amazing ability to intersperse his plots with nuggets of history and tradition of the lands where they unfolded in. He was a multi-faceted genius; but, coming from a line of distinguished raconteurs, he was at his skillful best when weaving magic through his stories.

Last year, I was unusually lucky. After years of longing, I finally got to visit the Corbett National Park. As a bonus, I also went to Jaisalmer – the setting of *Shonar Kella* (The Golden Fortress), a slightly average outing for Feluda the sleuth, but definitely one of the best ones for *Feluda* the traveler.

I did not come across a tiger in Corbett – we have murdered far too many of the royal beast for that. But the memory of the night that I spent there, still lingers on. Night, in the forest, can be all consuming. It is sudden and overpowering. Sound travels far and wide and the quietness of the immediate vicinity makes you hear things happening miles away. Sitting in front of a bonfire, as I stared fixedly at the embers and listened to the distant cries of the hyena, I was transported to a different time in a different age.

Jaisalmer evoked mixed feelings. The fort, with its dirty bylanes and stark realities of everyday life was quite an anticlimax. However, when I went a bit farther into the desert and looked back at a panoramic view of the fort, the romance of the situation was apparent. It stood proudly, on a natural elevation, bang in the middle of the Thar desert. Built of yellow sandstone, it glistened like gold under the desert sun. The imperiousness of the fort was accentuated several times over by the knoll it stood on and by the barenness of the desert all around. To me, it seemed like a proud chimney stretching into the sky. As I took in the grandeur, I could feel the valiance with which it repulsed the terrible siege that Alauddin Khilji had once laid on it. I was moved by the immense suffering that the inhabitants of the fort might have endured and was awed by the self-esteem of the women jumping to their *Jauhar*. At last, I knew why Jaisalmer would inspire *Ray*. It became clear to me, how this tale of poignance would find echo in the chief protagonist, *Mukul's*, enchanting visions of his past life.

Abhro da was certainly one of a kind, but others too were enlightened in their own ways. The desks that we sat on would be arranged in four different columns facing the teacher. One day when we were slightly older, our class teacher Mrs. Kelkar came in to find us arranged in a most unnatural way. Convenience had made us gravitate such that a overwhelming majority of the two columns on the right spoke Bengali, while a sizeable minority on the left spoke an assortment of languages other than Bengali. Mrs. Kelkar had split us up that day only to bring us a lot closer in the long run.

I think a lot of the openness was due to the breed of Fathers who ran our school then. Compared to some of the other schools around, habits were not imposed on us. We were free to converse in our vernacular tongues, and we gave as much importance to a Tagore or a

Premchand as we gave to a Wordsworth. Our Fathers were imbued by the missionary zeal but, when at school, their mission was to educate and not proselytize. They taught us that religion was a personal affair and we ought to respect an individual's faith. They showed us the value of not mixing religion with the secular aspects of life. It seemed natural to us that Swami Vivekananda could be given the same reverence as St. Ignatius Loyola or that pictures of the St. Xavier's Basilica should adorn the same walls as the Gomateshwar. We were taught to take pride in our identity, but also respect the differences in others.

It is true that we gained a lot by studying, but the learning was not always limited to books. Years later, when I got an insight into the pettiness of staff-room politics, my childhood role-models appeared crumbling. But when I thought about it deeper, it seemed hypocritical on my part to hold my teachers to a different yardstick than what I would do for myself. They were, after all, made of flesh and blood and could not have been perfect. And thus, I reasoned that their greatness lay in transcending the everyday trifles and holding before us ideals that we could aspire to follow.

5

THE MAN IN THE SHADOW OF
THE CHILD

The Pujas were, by far, the most awaited event on our annual calendar. Every year, around autumn, the air would be full of anticipation. Autumn represented a curious transition from the wetness of the monsoons to the chill of winter. At different times of the day, it would be both, but never quite one or the other. The sun would gradually get benign, the days shorter. The fans would rotate with much lesser intensity, yet we would not feel the need to snuggle under a blanket at night. Festive spirits would be high, with nature a willing ally. A sudden effusion of the white, velvety *kaash phool* would tell us that the time to invoke the Mother Goddess was near.

The days leading up to the Pujas would be full of activity – we would be in a lot of hurry to get things out of the way. Exams had to be finished; new clothes had to be bought. Those days, we were not in the habit of buying clothes throughout the year – most of our purchases happened during the Pujas. Thus, shopping for the Pujas, or 'marketing' as we called it, was every bit as important.

We would plan for the annual shopping trip, weeks in advance. It meant a rare evening out with the family. There were a few shops that we went to every year, and the shop-keepers knew us by name.

"*Didi*, this is the latest in fashion," – they would tell Mom.

To Dad, they would add – "*Dada*, it is quite reasonable!"

Branded clothes were rare and expensive – we would rather go for pieces of cloth to be later stitched into fashionable garments by the local tailor. Mom would go through the reams spread out by the shopkeeper and select the ones she thought would suit us the best. Our choice of clothes would be like our emotions – restrained in their expression. Occasionally, a brightly coloured piece of cloth would catch my eye, and Mom would disapprovingly say – "That's too gaudy!"

Getting something for all of us, would be a painstaking process. As Mom would go through the annual ritual, Dad would wait outside the shop with a disinterested look on his face. He knew he was there to provide financial support to the whole exercise but his mind would be elsewhere. Years later, on similar occasions like these, my wife, annoyed by my edginess, would remark how impatient I was when it came to shopping. It was true – I never quite enjoyed the experience. For me, the real joy would be the visit to the restaurant after the purchases were done. We did not eat out frequently, and as we sat sipping on bottles of Gold Spot, I would wish that the moment never ended. I would fool around with the narrow plastic pipe for a while, slurping on the drink, not wanting to finish too soon. I would hold the drink in my mouth, twirl my tongue around it and try to tame its sweet, cold fizz. Only when I had got the full import of its taste would I, slowly, unwillingly, swallow it. And, with each gulp, I would survey the amount left in the bottle and feel sad.

Every year, we would welcome the Pujas with the Mahalaya. Ma Durga, to us, was the personification of Shakti – the female energy. We loved her like family. The Mahalaya was when we would entreat her to take leave from her heavenly abode in Mount Kailash and come, stay with us. We would wake up, at the crack of dawn, to the deep, sonorous incantation on the radio:

Ya Devi sarva bhuteshu Matri rupena samsthita
Ya Devi sarva bhuteshu Shakti rupena samsthita
Ya Devi sarva bhutesu Shanti rupena samsthita
Namestasyai Namestasyai Namestasyai Namoh Namah!

There must have been something moving about the voice because AIR had been playing the same audio, with amazing consistency, for the past several decades and yet it sounded as fresh and as thrilling as ever. Coming just a week before the Pujas, the Mahalaya started the actual countdown to the D-Day.

From then on, it would be a mad rush against time. On the field in front of our house, the pandal-wallahs would be on overdrive, working throughout the night, to get the pandal ready on time. At night, we would go to sleep with the blazing halogen illuminating our bedroom and the sound of the vigorous hammering in the background. In the morning, we would go to school lamenting that it did not seem likely that the pandal would be ready on time. But, like all else Indian, things would magically fall into place at the last moment, and by Panchami, the tarpaulin would be stretched taut over the bamboo scaffolding. Her bivouac resplendent, we would eagerly wait for Ma to take her pride of place inside.

Ma Durga did not come alone. She would have her divine children Saraswati, Lakshmi, Ganesh and Kartik accompanying her. As an afterthought, we would also put a small portrait of her husband, Lord Shiva, at the top. With her family by her side and at peace in her maternal abode, she would have a kind and contented glow about her. Even with some of the fiercest weaponry on each of her ten hands and the slain demon-king Asur at her feet, she would have the look of mercy on her face. We were not afraid of her – to us, she was a gentle, motherly figure who had had to take up weapons to wipe off evil from the face of the earth. She was our saviour; she was one of our own.

There were a lot of people who took great care in the meticulous designing of their pandals and, in the process, elevated them to a marvelous art form. Some would be built as elaborate replicas of famous monuments, while others would be designed intricately from something as ordinary as match-sticks. Current affairs was a popular theme and some pandals, in the complexity of their designs, would provide a critic's commentary on the happenings around the world. The fame of pandals such as these would spread far and wide and they would see a steady stream of visitors throughout the day.

In contrast to the splendor on offer elsewhere, ours would be quite a modest effort. Ours was a close-knit community Puja to which barely anyone from outside ever came. Partly due to this and partly due to the fact that our pandal was the result of neighbourhood contributions, we had a very strong sense of attachment to it. Our Dads ran the entire show, making it very personal for us. The effort would be sans grandeur, but would be no less in passion. In overseeing the arrangements, they would so customize it that we kids had a hell of a time. They would make the Pujas special for us.

With the sound of the dhak, a barrel-shaped drum, sending a flutter through our hearts, the actual fanfare would commence on Shashthi and go on for the next four days. We would start off with the ritualistic offerings, but as the day progressed, we would gravitate increasingly towards the food stalls and the small dais adjacent to the pandal. This dais and the benches in front of it was the place where we would spend most of our Puja evenings. This was where we would have our extempore competitions, art contests and musical extravaganza. This was the place where our Dads envisioned that we would learn and hone some of our 'extra-curricular' skills. And, this was what made us cherish our Puja more than some of the more grandiose ones around.

The annual festivities would conclude on the day of the Vijaya Dashami. As the rest of India enthusiastically celebrated the triumph of good over evil, our hearts would be full of agony. For us, it would be the day when we had to bid farewell to Ma. It would also be the day of bidding goodbye to parental leniency and a return to the stringency of early-to-bed-early-to-rise-disobey-it-and-Dad'll-cut-you-down-to-size. With a hint of sorrow, we would think about the year of drudgery ahead only after which Ma would come again to lighten our lives. The more sentimental among us would sob a little. Though, as I sought blessings from Ma before seeing her off, I would, like an errant child, furtively hunt around for pieces of her tin-weaponry to keep as souvenirs.

We were remarkably nonchalant when it came to religion. It would thus seem odd that we placed such a great emphasis on the Durga Puja. But then, the Durga Puja was so much more than mere religion. It's true that we chanted Sanskrit slokas and worshipped the Goddess with all the necessary fervour, but that would hardly be the focal point. For me, it was always the fun. Through our extempore competitions and our art contests, we celebrated the spirit devoid of the dogma. By separating the dais from the pandal, we made the event a lot more inclusive.

The nature of the festival probably aided us in making it more liberal. Certain aspects of the Hindu religion are quite private. Prayer and worship, to us, are best left to the confines of our homes. The idea of communal worship is somewhat alien to our scriptures. Converting the Durga Puja into a form of communal worship was, thus, a critical departure from established norms. In doing so, the inventors of the 'community-*Puja*' were able to free themselves from the shackles of orthodoxy and introduce the element of 'society' that is so essential in bringing hearts together. If their effort was to ensure that a religious festival did not form the basis for another set of divisions, they were largely successful in this endeavour.

Above all, I look back at the Pujas with a lot of fondness for a very personal reason. When I was about twelve or thirteen, it was during the Pujas that I took my first diffident steps towards sexuality.

Teenage, to me, was hours of poring over the mirror desperately searching for something to be proud off, and getting dejected each time. When looking good was all that mattered, I found myself wanting in every respect. There were pounds of unwanted flesh at all the wrong places – should I suck in my belly and hold my breath? My shoulders weren't broad enough – how do I puff up my chest? I could be a tad taller – do I stand on my toes? Why didn't I have enough hair on my face – how would I fashion a French-beard? When did my voice become so slippery and why would it begin trembling at the most embarrassing of moments – will I never have a baritone? Oh, God! How could I ever get her to look at me!

Unlike other phases of my life, teenage did not start with a specific date or even a logical end. It was not like getting into school or coming out of college. On the contrary, it was a gradual change in body and mind, often too mild to take notice. While I was busy aping the battle of Kurukshetra with my crude, home-made bow & arrow, teenage seems to have tip-toed in and caught me unawares.

One of the very first changes that made me uncomfortable was an innate desire to impress the opposite sex. The world seemed my playground and every other female, a potential mate. With hormones on tenterhooks, I was liable to be hypersensitive in the presence of girls. Clumsiness would be a loyal companion as I went around making a fool of myself. In my eagerness to seek attention, I think I ended up raising quite a few eyebrows.

When I look back at those heady times, there are a whole lot of situations that I would not have wanted to find myself in. I particularly remember a rainy Sunday morning. Showers were unusual for that time of the year, and I had gone to the market without an umbrella. While I was coming back, the heavens suddenly gave way and thick drops of rain started pouring down with an increasing sense of purpose. As the rain gathered momentum, I dashed to the shade of the nearest banyan tree. With nothing better to do and cursing the rain as an unnecessary interference, I tried to keep myself busy with the empty polythene bag lying nearby. I was having a hard time trying to decipher the faded writing on the bag, when I noticed a movement from the corner of my eye. Up ahead, a couple of windows down the road, I saw her stare fixedly at the rain. She had just taken a bath, and with her wet, disheveled hair carelessly hanging by her shoulders, she looked stunning. I had always had a huge crush for Sumi and now was my time to show what I was made of. Bravado, I thought, would be a brilliant ploy to find my way into her heart and I looked around for suitable props. All that I could see in front of me was the dusty, faded poly bag. So, I picked it up, tore open one of the edges, covered my head with it and ventured out into the beating rain.

I made exaggerated moves in front of her window, stopping at times and looking sideways, with rehearsed inadvertence, to increase the dramatic effect. With the plastic bag half covering my eyes I could not see clearly, but I could definitely make out the disinterested look on her face. She barely noticed my theatricals for a while before disappearing. And, I was left there like a fool nursing his pride. The plastic bag was a face saver – it provided a modicum of privacy to what otherwise felt like public humiliation.

In short, this was to be my fate during teenage years. I would devise one ridiculous scheme after another and get rebuffed every time. I would look at my ugly awkwardness against her feline grace and knew that she was not for me. And yet, I would persevere in the faint hope that she would, one day, be moved by my efforts and give me a smile of approval. Sumi was no ordinary girl. She was, to me, what perfection looked like. Her presence would make me anxious and fill me with a rush of emotions, the likes of which I had never experienced before. She would make my life meaningful in those years of aimlessness.

Sumi had a round face with big, almond eyes that did all the talking. They would flit around carelessly, as if unaware of the spell that they cast over me. There would be something wild and untamed about them that I would find intensely alluring. She would giggle a lot and her pink, bow-shaped lips would part to reveal a row of flashing, white teeth neatly arranged with her cheeks bulging out like huge scoops of ice-cream. Her smile would be precious in its unpredictability – the most trivial of things would make her laugh and yet the most substantial of efforts would go unnoticed. Her mischievous coquettishness would drive me crazy and with her long, shapely arms her smooth, artistic fingers and her wildly swaying pony-tail, she would be like a maestro conducting a grand orchestra of the enraptured.

I think our first meeting set the tone of our future interactions. I distinctly remember that it was one of the Puja days and she was wearing a brilliant blue silk blouse with a jet-black skirt that accentuated her curves. It was her birthday and after a lot of deliberation, I had mustered enough courage to bring along a red rose with a silver foil carefully wrapped around the stem. I remember I had gone to great lengths and rehearsed my lines umpteen times. But once inside the pandal, and in front of so many prying eyes, I lost heart. She stood at an arm's length, probably expecting me to make the first move, and all that I could manage were a few unsure steps and a sort of confused, dazed look on my face. For, while going through what I would say to her, I had not anticipated how I should convey the most private of feelings in the most public of places.

So, I stood transfixed, feeling let down by the din around. The loudspeaker was a particular irritant. It was belting out a typically suggestive Bollywood number, meticulously chosen to be so inappropriate for the moment. The song had something to do about the quest for the unknown. The female requested secrecy; in a husky tone, she pleaded – "*Gupt! Gupt!*" Undeterred, the resolute male kept pressing, exploring the idea further. He started singing about undulations, of hills and trenches while the female kept imploring him to be more discreet.

And, in the boldness of the celluloid couple, my timidity got overlooked forever.....

Teenage was not all about love; it was a lot about lust too. While love was important, the act of making love was quite significant as well. But, in my world, real-life sexual encounters were scarce at that age. Thus, I had to fall back on voyeurism and the virility of imagination to make up for the increasing urge of physical proximity. The female form, then, became an object of unusual obsession.

Television, those days, meant the Doordarshan and Doordarshan meant people like Dad running shows under a strict censorship regime. MTV was just making a tentative appearance in some homes, but was generally looked down upon as an avenue of abject lewdness. We had not subscribed to MTV, but armed with a metallic ladle and a screw-driver, I would find ways to take a peek into the forbidden world. Despite privacy being a luxury in my small, three-roomed house, I would find opportunities to watch music videos where women, unimaginably sexy, found it convenient to sing mournful songs about treachery and love while being naked to the waist. Quite annoyingly though, they would have their backs towards me. In their mournful tone, they would suggest that the world was not fair and I, doing a delicate balancing act with the ladle and eagerly putting up with their insipid poetry in the faint hope that they would turn towards me at least once, would seem to concur.

Books, as always, would be companions of choice. I would read about Tom's escapades as he went around whitewashing walls and planting kisses on Becky. Every once in a while there would these passages which would talk about breasts that smelled like jasmine or breaths that got smothered by kisses. I would stumble upon these jewels with the serendipity of a bounty hunter and read and re-read them till it seemed like the act was being played out just before my eyes. I would grow stiff, spend myself against the pillow and wonder about the liberated worlds that they dwelt in.

The eroticism would spill over to other facets of my life as well. The Biology text-book, with its graphic depiction of the female anatomy, would be a trusted alibi but even the Physics book could be of help at times. Often, a statement as innocuous as – "a proton is a hydrogen atom STRIPPED OFF its lone electron" – could set my pulse racing! On wintry mornings, I would blow my warm breath on the cold window pane, proceed to draw the female form on the mist formed and then keep marveling at my creation.

Yes, in that repressed age, when emotions were eager to burst out, we had to dig into our reserves.

When I evaluate my adolescent years, I think I did just about average. Theory suggested that I should have fared better, but evidence proved otherwise. A twin sister, with her all-girl friend circle, should have given me easy access to a fertile catchment area from where to build upon. But, in the cloistered environment of a 'boys only' school, we were handicapped in our ability to strike up a normal conversation with a girl without getting self-conscious. It did not matter when we were kids, but as we grew up, this under-preparedness rankled deep inside. Society was not of much help either. In my immediate vicinity boy-girl relationships were frowned upon as unnecessary diversions and were the source of much gossip. All in all, the surroundings were such that only the more socially gifted thrived, and guys like me, got left behind.

Having said this, I do not think that those impetuous years were any less useful for me as for any other. I think their usefulness lay in making me aware of my self, of my abilities and my shortcomings. In introducing an element of self-doubt, I think they made me take a more realistic assessment of things. In confronting me with my sexuality and its associated emotions, they ensured that the world would never be as simple and as carefree again. In a sense, they made the kid grow up.

To add to it were the inevitable questions of deference to authority. As a kid, I had toed the parental line without any misgivings. Adolescence taught me to judge people and events on their own merit without getting swayed by conventional wisdom. The world was suddenly not black and white but varying shades of grey.

I look back at adolescence with a touch of fondness for having taught me some of the most important lessons of life. It is, thus, somewhat ironic that the end was not as well as the beginnings were. Towards the close, my teens were marred by a terrible personal tragedy that would change my life forever.

6
LIFE AFTER DEATH

It was a dull, grey Tuesday morning. The quietness was ominous and hung heavy, like the all-too-familiar lull before the storm. Our Board Exams were just a week away and my sister and I were up before the sun, busy giving finishing touches to our preparations. There were last year's question papers to go through, the odd loose end on the Indian freedom struggle to tie, the critic's summary of *As You Like It* to read up, a little bit of Mathematics to practice – in short, a mountain of small tasks that had been gathering dust till the last minute.

It was a regular day for Dad as well. He woke up around five, brushed his teeth and filled up the vessels with the early morning supply of municipal water. He then picked up the cup of tea that Mom had prepared before, hovered around our study room for a

while unsure of how to share the burden of thoughts weighing him down, before getting engrossed in the day's news in *The Statesman*. He spent about an hour lapping up the different articles and pieces of incisive analyses, murmured with disgust at the latest scam unfolding before the nation and seemed slightly concerned by the increasing tide of insularity in national politics. With a degree of prophecy, he remarked, "The future does not look bright at all!"

Close to seven, he got up from his chair and got ready to go to office. There was only a slight departure from the usual routine. He told Mom –

"I need to come back early today. I won't be taking my bike to work."

With that he trudged out – the slow, painful gait of a sickly man going to his doom. Incidentally, that would be the last time he set foot from home.

Dad had a remarkable amount of willpower. A chain smoker, he could be quite cavalier when it came to health. As a pernicious combination of tobacco and hereditary ailments kept steadily gnawing at his physical strength, he would will himself to hold out a bit longer. He would reason with friends and family that he did not yet, want to go to the doctor and cause unnecessary fuss just before the Boards. From destiny, he had probably begged for a month's respite beyond which he would be diligent in attending to his failing health.

Unfortunately, fate did not afford him that luxury.

That day, he did not come back home, as promised.

At about eleven in the morning, we got an anxious call from one of our neighbours that Dad was extremely unwell – at office, he had complained of severe chest pain and had to be rushed to the hospital. We knew how Dad felt about going to the hospital, and we feared the worst. I looked at Mom – she was completely stone faced and kept muttering to herself, "It can't be. It can't be!"

~

The next few hours were a haze of false hopes, depressing reality and ultimately a state of denial.

~

Once at the hospital, the funereal atmosphere hit me. It was a government-run organization – a far cry from the sophisticated private ones that we see all around us today. The corridors were dank and dimly lit, the doors and windows were a dull yellow and thick with ages of dust, the strong, unpleasant odour of disinfectant overpowered the senses. There was a baby wailing nearby and a row of curious onlookers milling around taking a perverse pleasure at our misery. When psychological strength was all that you needed, the hospital, with its moroseness let you down badly. The truth was harsh but irrefutable – you knew that it was a place you did not come out alive from.

Dad was an unfamiliar sight. Unconscious, helpless and a shadow of his usual feisty self, he lay there on the bed, surrounded by friends and colleagues. All of a sudden, he looked thin, emaciated and a lot older. With his right hand he clutched at his chest, from which emerged a handful of electrodes that were trying to keep track of a faint, erratic heartbeat. There were drops of red on the side of his mouth – his friends explained, wishfully, that it was from the red syrup that the doctor had given him earlier. We were only too eager to believe that.

Mom sat by the bed, shocked by the incomprehensibility of this sudden turn of events. Was it not just a couple of hours back that Dad had left home, as usual, seemingly hale and hearty? Was it not a mere fortnight when Mom had, like other women, prayed for her husband's longevity during Shiv-ratri? Was it not untimely and unjust for something like this to happen with two kids in school and one barely in his twenties? What had she done to deserve it?

Yes, there were a lot of unanswered questions in our minds. The world felt cruel. The future looked bleak. But we were not ready to come to terms with it yet. For, imperceptible though it was, the heart was still beating.

In his failing battle with life, Dad would snatch a few precious moments of victory. Like tenacious shrubs on a hopelessly barren land, his prolonged state of delirium would be dotted with characteristic fortitude and concern for our well being. One moment he would talk about riding a rickshaw with his long departed parents in tow, another moment he would be asking for his spectacles to read the next morning's newspaper. For most of the time, he would have a lost, hollow look on his face; but, there would also be brief periods of coherence when he would look at Mom with a touch of guilt.

At about four, the next morning, he breathed his last. A couple of paces down the room where he lay was the maternity ward from where, only fifteen years ago, he had come out beaming – the proud father of a recently born pair of twins. Fifteen years later, he came out draped in white. For a man who was all logic, he was surprisingly superstitious about the auspiciousness of Wednesday. Ironically, it was an early Wednesday morning that he embarked on his arduous journey to the afterlife.

In death, he looked a picture of tranquility. Eyes firmly shut; there was the hint of a calm smile on his face. His hands lay by his sides, palms slightly bent at the wrist, the head raised a bit upwards and the lips curved like a tiny 'o'. It seemed that life had deserted him through the mouth.

We received the news with stunned silence. It seemed impossible that we would never see him walk again. It seemed impractical that our lives could go on without him guiding and protecting us. Dad had been like a giant banyan tree sheltering us from the vagaries of nature, while Mom had nurtured and nourished us in his shade. With him gone, it seemed that the roof had been torn apart, leaving us vulnerable to the forces of destiny. Mom was inconsolable – she had lost a dear friend and companion with whom she had shared a better part of her adult life. Now that he had left her so abruptly, there was very little for her to look forward to. And yet, even in her profound grief, there were more practical considerations to worry about. A novice when it came to matters outside home, she did not have the faintest idea how she would manage with three young kids, all by herself. More immediately, with relatives still on their way and a dead husband waiting for his final rites to be performed by the eldest son studying in far-away Varanasi, she could not afford to be consumed by her loss. Suddenly, she felt very lonely.

However, we were not quite alone in our bereavement. My uncle had already come in the night before and was now tending to all the logistics that the dead needed to start on their long voyage. As he did so, memories of childhood flashed in his mind and brought a few private tears to his eyes. Moreover, in the absence of other members of the extended family, our neighbours had readily stepped into the void. They were men with whom Dad had shared many a light moment, women who had spent hours with Mom and children whom we had grown up with. In our moment of miserable sorrow, in our craving for shoulders to cry on, they stood by us quite like the way they had done in happier days. When nature seemed wicked and selfish, they came in with their kindred spirits to help sustain our wavering belief in life.

⌒

It was almost night, when we started for the cremation grounds. News had already reached brother who, in his urgency, had chosen the unlikeliest of modes to travel across three hundred miles of the dark, treacherous G.T. Road on his way home. Throwing caution to the winds, he had hired a local cab – but, what good were concerns for personal safety when all that mattered was the proximity to near and dear ones!

We met up at the cremation site by the Damodar river. Originating in the Chhotanagpur Plateau, the Damodar is one of the many rivers that feed into the Bhagirathi, tributary of the Ganga. As the Giver of Life and the Purgatory of Sins, the Ganga is quite seminal to Hinduism. And, by virtue of its linkage to the great river, the Damodar too represents an easy ascent to heaven. Having lived my entire life in Durgapur, it was, thus, peculiar that I had never before stood on the banks of the 'sorrow of Bengal' that had a reputation for causing devastating floods. And there, by the Damodar, at the dead of night and with Dad being made ready for the funeral pyre, we wept together like we had never done before.

Brother looked at the lifeless form lying beside and tried to comfort me. With tears rolling down his cheeks, he said in a trembling voice – "I am here. Don't cry!". And, with that, the kid who was still a boy was once again pushed into becoming a man, much before his time.

As for me, I looked at Dad and let out a long sigh. Before the wanton flames turned flesh and blood to ashes, I longed for one last moment in which to bid him a decent goodbye. I longed to assuage his guilt-ridden conscience; I longed to tell him –

"Don't worry Dad; you've done a fine job. It's up to us now!"

Though, the import of the damage was not immediately apparent, Dad, in his untimely departure, had left behind a very real hole in our lives. For almost a month after his death, we were in a daze, mechanically going through all the necessary customs and rituals. Uncles and aunts had arrived, and their soothing presence, like opium, made us overlook our anguish. It was only when they started going back to their own lives that the enormity of the situation became evident. In the bike that remained idle, in the slippers that remained crossed, in the spectacles that remained folded, in the tunes that Mom never hummed again, in every small bit that was or wasn't the same we came to realize that our lives, as we knew it, had changed forever. In a sense, it was like turning the page of a book with the knowledge that you could not turn it back again.

Dad, for us, was a memory frozen in time.

Despite the gloom that had felt immovable then, our lives went on. And, gradually, over many a tearful day, we came to terms with our sorrow. Through the many years that have since passed, we have chosen to bury the darkness of that day as a nightmare, best forgotten. They say that the soul is immortal – I think Dad lives in our thoughts and actions, to this very day. It is true that the physical features of his person have become somewhat fuzzy, but his ideas are as fresh as ever.

When I look at myself, Dad's impact becomes preeminent. He was a strong personality with a bunch of clearly cut beliefs. But, what made him stand apart in my eyes was his rational self and dispassionate application of logic, especially when it came to people. He was not the one to be swayed by the intensity of emotion and colour men in black or white. Rather, he would be of the opinion that individuals were rarely totally good or bad and one could always find a reason why a person acted in a particular manner under a given set of circumstances. He would be unbiased in the application of this yardstick and would usually be fair in his assessment of people and their motives. Thus, he could find something right in the fiercest of opponents or something wrong in the most loyal of supporters.

This rationality extended to his religious beliefs as well. He was not much for the ceremony of religion. True faith, he felt, was intensely personal and did not need the appurtenances of fanfare. "Be good and do good", he would say, "and, you would not feel the need to go to a temple." In spite of this, he would never stand in the way of belief. I remember the Saraswati Pujas at home. He would be assiduous in the arrangements that Mom needed, but would be busy with the newspaper when the actual offerings were being made.

And thus, free of all edicts issued by 'holy men', he would develop a very deep distaste for those who mixed religion with politics. To him they were like fuel and fire – a dangerous recipe with disastrous consequences. He would say that religion in politics was like a smoke screen that the dubious used either to whip up mass hysteria or pander to their selfish vote banks, all the while masking the real issues at hand.

Unsurprisingly, politics could evoke very strong reactions from Dad – maybe, it was just the passion of defending the indefensible. A die-hard Leftist, much of his youth was spent as an active party worker and much of his later years in apologetic defence of his choices. Politics, as we know in India, has long been dominated by questions of class, caste, language and religion. Of all the splinters that these have given rise to, none has been as inflexible in their ideology as the Leftists, the champions of class-based struggle. Impervious to influence, ethical or unethical and convinced of their intellectual superiority, they have zealously forwarded the cause of the needy, often placing themselves in impractical positions vis-à-vis prevailing economic wisdom. True, their advocacy of land reforms has benefited the landless labourer. Significant still, these positive strides in rural society have helped temper the ills of feudalism for a large cross section of rural India. In other areas the Left have, like the Right, been less prone to hero-worship and dynastic politics. And, unlike the Right, they have also been able to maintain religious harmony.

However, in their dogged fight against class inequalities, they have so defined themselves on the basis of vehement and relentless opposition to authority through slogans like "*dhuan bandh, chakka bandh*" (chimneys won't burn, wheels won't turn), that governance has been an unfortunate casualty. Even more far-reaching and unfortunate has been their subtle impact on the Bengali psyche that has, over a period of time, tended to look down upon the creation and the creator of wealth, in general. Lopsided, thus in focus and uncompromising on ideology, they have found it difficult to justify their economic and urban failures against their social and rural accomplishments. To sum up, success has been a story easily sold in the villages but had always needed some stretch of imagination in the cities.

Today, I can hardly reconcile myself to the fact that a man, so thoroughly rational otherwise, could for years be deluded by some irrelevant concern about "imperialism in Peru", while the termite of militant trade unionism wasted commerce and industry at home. When Dad was alive, our political exchanges would mostly be passionate monologues – my concepts were ill-formed and I would listen attentively to his espousal of the policies of the Left. I wonder if he would have been as passionate today. I wonder how he would have felt at the alienation of industry that keeps his son far away from home. I wonder if he would have called it a 'historic blunder'!

Yes, my father was like everyone else – a man of flesh and blood with his folly and his astuteness. And then, as now, I aspired to be like him.

7
THE TEMPLES OF LEARNING

*T*rrrrrrrring......

The shrill, unruliness shattered my precious early morning slumber. I woke up with a start and desperately looked around for the source of this ear-splitting noise. Jolted by the unexpected din, I thought to myself – it must be that clunky alarm-clock again! It has to be that slimy, bastard Sundar!

The alarm-piece in question was an object of terror. Hyper-charged by a row of batteries, it was an abominable invention, the loudness of whose alarm was only matched by the irritating '*tick-tick*' that it did while running. It was custom made to strike at the heart of torpor. The inventor was probably an insomniac or maybe just a misanthrope.

In the hands of Sundar, the clock was like a weapon of mass deprivation. He had this eccentric idea that if the alarm went off anywhere near his reach he could just bang it off and go back to sleep. So, it had to be at a sufficient distance for him to make all the effort to reach out and cajole it to quietness. Thus, he reasoned, the last traces of sleep would be wiped away from his weary eyes.

It was a revolutionary thought and, though mildly idiotic, Sundar had a firm belief in its efficacy. Every night, before going off to bed, he would hunt for ever more challenging places to hide it in, making it more and more impractical for anybody to find it the next morning. Inevitably, when morning came, faced with the enormity of the task, he would be the first to bury his ears deep into the pillow – leaving us to heap the most imaginative of insults on the faithful clock, its hapless inventor and Sundar's non-existent sister.

Last night, the slimy bugger must have slipped it into my room!

With the alarm reaching its crescendo, I wriggled with discomfort for a while. Finally, I got up, shut up the impertinent timekeeper and grumbled out of my room with half-open eyes. Along the way, I landed a vicious kick on the closed doors of Sundar's room and mouthed a few more curses.

It was just another morning at Vidya Mandir.

Vidya Mandir, or VM as we fondly referred to it, was somewhat of an abnormality. In a country where investment in education is an afterthought and educational institutions are personal fiefdoms of the politically connected, VM received a lavish grant from the government and a fair degree of autonomy to spend the money as it desired. It was an 'institute of excellence' – an elusive dream for students all over the nation, especially those from the dusty provinces.

As if to live up to its name, VM had designed a grueling selection process that was meant to look down on our abilities. Year after year, hundreds of thousands would compete and only a few would make the cut. Alluring as the dream was, it had spawned a whole industry in its wake. There would be institutes like assembly line factories, which trained you to get into VM, and there would be other institutes that trained you to get into those assembly line factories.

It was a costly, attritional race. For hours we would agonize over problems that had tenuous ties with our everyday lives. In our wonderlands, ants would spring up magically at the vertices of equilateral triangles and start walking with the sole objective of meeting up at the centre. They would be tricksters with minds of their own and ever so often looked at each other and changed their paths slightly – and, we would be left wracking our brains trying to infuse some mathematical sense into their randomness.

In some sense, this was symptomatic of the way that we would act in our pursuit of the mirage. VM would be our single-minded obsession and we, like ants, would come from different corners of the country aiming to converge onto the oasis of exclusivity that Pandit Nehru, in a moment of typical poetic flourish, had named as "the temple of learning".

☞

Thus, we came to VM, and we came in droves. We came from Bengal, Andhra, from Gujarat, from the Punjab. We came from towns, cities and villages – from lands much venerated, as also from nooks totally obscure. Most defining, however, was the fact that whether prince or pauper, we all came through the grind of hard labour – in a country where the high and mighty call all the shots, it was an achievement of sorts.

☞

My first meeting with Sundar was somewhat erotic. I still remember the day we were spread out in an irregular semi-circle in the hostel 'games room'. The table tennis board had been cleared and at the centre were a handful of over-zealous 'seniors' eager to rub our noses into the ground. We were numerically superior, several times over, but the balance of power rested firmly with them. They were seasoned campaigners united in their resolve while we were disparate elements trying to find our feet. An age-old deference to hierarchy further cemented their invincibility. VM authorities had, on the pain of summary expulsion, banned all forms of 'ragging', but, as was evident, the ingenious could still find newer, more imaginative avenues of humiliation.

With casual arrogance, they called me to the centre. Beside me was a healthy-looking lad, with slightly puffy cheeks. His spectacles ate up a large portion of his face; and despite the squareness of its glasses and the gaudiness of its bright red, he looked at home. He wore a bright yellow shirt, a pair of blue denim and a couple of spotless white sneakers. In the cacophony of his colours, Sundar was just waiting to be ambushed. They called him as well.

The brief was explicit and demeaning. Sundar had to stand behind me and mime a vigorous to and fro motion, while I had to moan lustily and parrot out the cheap parody of a yesteryear *Bollywood* blockbuster. So, as he went back and forth like a man on a mission, I mustered all the sensuousness and begged for mercy. I panted –

"*Kam Maaro Kammmmmmmmmm......*"

Rites of initiation over, we were welcomed with varying degrees of openness.

Our hostel had a vertebral arrangement with rows of rooms branching out from a central spine that ran from one end to the other. Each row made up a 'wing' and a bunch of 'wings', one on top of the other, made a 'block'. Mostly symmetrical, there was enough asymmetry in the structure to 'incentivize' the industrious. For, though the rooms were universally unimaginative and modest, there were some 'wings' which were clearly more preferred. They either provided an unobstructed view of the horizon or boasted of precious blandishments, like a hammock, for instance. The rest were those, maybe a tad lesser than equal that neither received direct sunlight nor were strategically located vis-à-vis the games room. They reveled in their facelessness.

Allotment to the wings was on the basis of an unwritten truism – the more influential you were, the better one you got. Of course the seniors, by virtue of familiarity, would get the best but if you were close enough, you too could find yourself significantly better off than your mates. And thus, the wing where you lived often determined the degree of control that you wielded. I lived in one that was neither too much to the centre, nor too much on the periphery.

The first few days at VM were a maze of emotions – there were the sudden pangs of loneliness, the urgency of setting up a home away from home and the discomfort of having to share space with individuals that were so different in their ways. It was also the time for re-assessing how much one was willing to do and how far one wanted to go.

I had always regarded myself as ambitious. While my friends at school had tended to take it easy, I had slogged to get into VM. It was, thus, quite a rude shock to find myself amidst people who had worked as hard, if not harder. What was more sobering was the feeling that a significant few of them, were not done yet. They hungered for more.

Sundar was from the coastal town of Vishakapatnam. He had spent most of his childhood there, but later, on finding the lazy paradise inadequate for his grand dreams, he had moved to Hyderabad. At Hyderabad, he had lived the life of an ascetic with his goal in sight and his books for company. Unlike some of his less motivated mates, he had not found time to catch a movie or a decent meal – indeed, he had run through many a night on a meager diet of instant noodles. Life had been a long, exciting race for him – a race where he had never come second, a race where he had combined the ferocity of a sprinter with the tenacity of a marathon-runner. This insatiable appetite for success and a string of favourable results had made him secure in his infallibility. He knew he was the best; he was convinced what he was getting was just not good enough. Despite being much ahead than the rest of us, he would often quarrel with life for not being fair to him. In his mind, circumstances were always conniving to keep him away from his dreams.

To me, VM was the culmination of my efforts. To *Sundar*, it was just another milestone. His brother had already traversed this route before and, while following his footsteps, he wanted to go much beyond. I had come to VM with the vague notion of being a 'scientist'. Unlike Sundar, I did not have my future charted out before me. While he planned for the next ten years, I was happy to look no farther than two. Thus, it was slightly uncomfortable when, on the third day at VM, he inquired –

"So, what do you want to become in life?"

Forced into unknown territory, I had ventured –

"Hmmm…I want to become an astronomer. I want to work at *ISRO*, the Indian Space Agency."

With a whole lot of incredulity, he had remarked –

"Why go to *ISRO*, if you can go to *NASA!*"

He had a point, but he definitely made me more confused. Since childhood, I had been conditioned to get into VM and be 'established'. Nobody had ever told me what to do after making it to VM. Thus, while VM was a tangible goal that I could work towards, 'being established' was much more abstract. Consequently, I had a hard time deciding how I should take my life forward. Rudderless, I thought it best to follow the herd – one day I would be on my path to becoming a 'scientist' while on another I would want to sell soaps.

I drifted around like a log of wood till, many years later, I finally found my calling. But, by then, I was way down a different route and would almost require an inhuman effort to re-align my course.

Meanwhile, during those formative days, I found myself alone in testy waters. Faced with the tremendous strength of clarity that people like *Sundar* possessed, and considering my own indecisiveness, I felt quite helpless. As always, I looked towards my teachers, the professors at VM. They were some of the leading luminaries in their field of work but, at the same time, a bit ill-equipped to address the more pertinent issue – the question of how to maintain our focus, exhausted as we were from the energy-sapping selection process that VM had put us through. Where some earnest nudging could have steered us in the right direction, we only got half-measures. For, it is true that VM had designated 'advisors'; but they prescribed more than they counseled – it certainly did not help that their prescriptions were often pontifical and at times insipid. What we were looking for, was somebody who would understand rather than evaluate – we were probably looking for some fatherly figures. And, in the absence of credible support, it gradually dawned on us that we were now grown up and had to fend for ourselves. Each of us reacted to this realization in our own way. While the determined kept up their steady progress, the more delicate turned into nervous wrecks. Once more, even in the super-charged atmosphere at VM, the vortex of ambition had separated the wheat from the chaff. This time, I found myself on a side that was less than flattering.

Within a short span of a few weeks, I became convinced that the rigour of academics was not for me. From then on, I would just do enough to see through the courses, while setting my sight on landing a cushy job at the end of my stint. I told myself that depth of knowledge was not a pre-requisite for a 'successful' career. Coming from somebody who had always held books in awe, it was no mean transformation.

VM was the favourite hunting ground for companies looking for achievers. What you knew mattered, but your grades mattered more; what mattered the most, however, was the manner you presented yourself. In that, the city-boys stole a march.

Ashish was from the grand-daddy of all cities, Delhi. The only son of a high-flying bureaucrat, he had had a privileged upbringing. He had attended the most snobbish of schools that had polished and smoothened him for a bright future. Adept in his use of cutlery, discerning in his differentiation of a 'pastry' from a 'cake' and at-ease with a large audience listening to him speak, he was the perfect recipe for drooling blue-chip executives. Life had been easy for him, and with the precious set of skills he had acquired, he knew that the future would be even easier.

In all his refinement, he was a formidable impediment for Sundar. Sundar knew that he had started his race a couple of paces behind and would have to double his efforts to catch-up. Though cordial to each other, there would be a sense of understated rivalry whenever the two were around.

Of all the things that *Ashish* was bothered about, shoes were his primary concern. He would spend an inordinate amount of time polishing them. With a measure of philosophy, he would opine –

"A man is known by his shoes…"

Sundar would inspect the worn out pair that he was wearing and snap –

"Yes, maybe in the army!"

As for me, I could see the definite advantage that Ashish held and would try to emulate him – a sort of cheap imitation of the original. He moved around in hip circles, most definitively identified by their choice of music. In my eagerness to move up the social ladder and be accepted, music, I thought, would be the most effective prop. For, music divided us like nothing else did.

Fed on a heavy dose of Bollywood, music was a serious affair to me. In my kind of music, fifty-year olds wrote flowery paeans about teenage love, that forty-year olds would croon, while thirty-year olds brought it alive through their vigorous gyrations and pelvic thrusts on screen. My kind of music was binary in emotions – you were either effusive in praise of the beloved or mournful with the pain of unrequited love. My music did not teach me flippancy – it taught me reverence and hyperbole.

Ashish's taste, thus, struck me as fundamentally opposed to my sensibilities. It was a totally new experience that celebrated irreverence and had strong anti-establishment feelings at heart. In his world, personalities and their songs dealt with a whole lot of issues other than love. They were bards singing about the inevitability of change, traitors that denounced war and empathized with the enemy, proud soldiers of the confederacy that eulogized the southern way of life, carefree souls that argued forcefully for the primacy of the individual, and others that were just angry, pretentious and high on dope.

Listening to that kind of music was a strange sensation. The feelings were pertinent and the causes seemed noble; but the emotions were peculiarly alien and difficult to relate to. While the highest forms of my music were a saccharine blend of serenity and senility, his music was mostly about youth and raw energy. While the vocalist received undivided adulation in my world, the guitarist was equally important in his scheme of things.

Above all, music gave me the sliver of an opening into the closed doors of his society; and, I was determined to 'head-bang' my way to the innermost circles. Armed with a bottle of beer and affected mouthing of some of the most popular lyrics, I barged in. Through the night I banged my head with gusto and went into a delusional trance induced by *Psychedelia*. In the morning, I woke up to a heavy hangover, a stiff neck and the door as firmly shut as ever.

Sundar had no time for charades.

After a typically frustrating night of fruitless buffoonery, I burst into his room only to find him lying on the bed. With his forearm half shading his eyes, he seemed to be levitating. A soft, slow Chinese song playing in the background was the apparent reason for his abnormal lightness. He had downloaded the song the night before and had put it on infinite loop. It had slowly grown on him and he was now transported to the world of bamboo shoots and paddy fields. With misty eyes, he spoke from a strange, faraway land. He said – "Hmmmm…You know, it reminds me of the momo stall by my home…."

Pissed off with another luckless night, I retorted with contempt – "Well, the Chinese do not eat momos. It probably was a guy from Sikkim!"

Shocked out of his stupor, he casually remarked – "Ah, much ado about nothing. They are all the same!"

Unusually aggressive, I pressed on – "Indeed, they are all the same! Is that what they teach you in Madras?"

Barely hiding his anger, he said, "I am not from Madras. Hell! I'm not even from Tamil Nadu. You 'northies' are so typical!"

Infuriated by now, I shouted – "Fucker! You do know that I am from the east!"

And, so we went around in circles, till we realized that we were not making much headway. Both of us were just being stubborn and refused to see logic. I scowled at him and left in a huff.

I was waging an uphill battle of acceptance, but I was certainly not alone in that endeavour.

Niru, the young woman from Bokaro, just went by her first-name. While a kid, her father had done away with the latter half in an apparent effort to wipe off the stigma of caste in a stiflingly casteist society. Her mother had further demolished all stereotypes when she had plodded her to get educated and become independent. Oblivious of all the insinuations that society made, Niru had toiled hard to get recognition on her own merit. While girls her age had obsessed about the colour of nail paint or the brand of 'fairness cream' she had busied herself in a much more meaningful life. She wanted to make a career and such frivolities had no place in her world. She had competed with boys on equal terms and beaten them comfortably. She had a promising future to look forward to – a future where she would be successful among people who would respect her abilities. She hoped to get her due at VM.

Unfortunately, she had misjudged the baggage that a lot of us came with. For, irrespective of the places we came from, our subconscious minds imagined women in a particular place with a particular role to perform – none of which had anything remotely connected with independence. Thus, seeing women like Niru was a rude awakening. In our feudalistic make-up we could not accept the fact that Niru was as able as we were. We did not deem it fit to judge her by what she had achieved rather than by how she looked.

In our minds, the ideal woman ought to be 'fair', 'beautiful' and 'homely'. She had to be submissive and acquiesce to the pleasures of her man. She was an object of recreation and procreation. Niru with her strong-willed independence was, thus, ill-equipped to deal with a 5000 year old diktat. It was not in her to be a dainty daisy. Through our pointed barbs about her ungainliness, the inadequacy of her sexual organs or the supposed looseness of her morals, we made her know that.

At first, Niru could only muster scorn. She knew that she was at VM because of her brains and not because of how she looked. She reacted in the only manner that she knew – she fought hard. But faced with tremendous odds of twenty-to-one and no motherly shoulder for support, she eventually thought of compromise. Maybe, a cigarette in hand and some generous use of swear-words would gain her the acceptance that she craved for. Maybe that was the only way to gain a foothold in a traditionally male bastion.

And thus, Niru and I took our own tentative steps towards acceptance. We were unsuccessful in various measures, and over a period of time we realized that blind emulation would not work. There was much that we could appreciate in each other and much that we could critique. It was beneficial in adopting what was good, but we certainly did not need an approval to establish our worth. We understood that the only way to gain respect was to interact on an equal footing. If we did not respect ourselves, no amount of acceptance could make us feel good.

This realization was essential and it eventually enabled us to be part of one seamless group without necessarily having to suppress our individualities. And that enhanced the group as well.

VM was set in idyllic surroundings away from the temptations of city life. A solitary railway track ran by its boundary, occasionally reminding us of human habitation that lay far beyond the horizon. In so designing it, the founding fathers had hoped that the tranquility would spur the mind on its quest for knowledge. They had imagined students as hermits with little time for worldly pleasures. Understandably, they fell woefully short of providing enough for a crowd to which knowledge was secondary. They did have a theatre that ran movies well past their sell-by date, and free internet that could be used for porn; but, that was about all.

Ashish often complained about the lack of 'night-life' at VM. Back home, I had seldom been up after ten and the concept of night-life was quite foreign. Maybe he felt the pinch more or maybe he liked to be in the thick of things; whatever the reason, he was not content with cribbing about the problem, he wanted to be the solution as well. Disadvantage often brings out the best in the resourceful; and Ashish was nothing, if not resourceful.

Before long, he decided what the best use of his time would be. There were quiz contests to be conducted, music competitions to be arranged, athletics championships to be organized – a plethora of activities that would keep his nights busy and make his life livelier. Suddenly, VM did not seem so dull anymore.

Someone with a lot of foresight and a degree of Ashish's restlessness had designed the annual extra-curricular calendar at VM. Throughout the year, there would be different events where hostels would compete with each other – the grand prize being the General Championships Trophy at the end of the term. Carefully combining sports and culture, with a dash of literature thrown in, the events were chosen to appeal to a diverse cross-section among us. Very few would come in with a natural edge; rather, the events themselves would be an opportunity to pick up new skills. Each individual event would be important; but against the unfolding drama of the race to the jackpot, some would be even more significant. Every single win or loss altered the points table setting in motion a furious bout of calculations, strategies and counter strategies.

Of all the events in the calendar, none was as remarkable as the Rangoli contest. It was an event that would involve all of us – the talented few with their creativity and the rest of us with our enthusiasm. It would be the most draining and the most fulfilling of all. Held during Diwali each year, it was a grand contest that involved decorating the considerable façade of the hostels with earthen lamps and Rangoli. We would take our decorations mostly from mythology – though, at times, we would also try to put across social messages. We got credit for the ideas, as well as their execution.

It was my last Rangoli at VM, when Syed finally made his mark. A man of extra-ordinary talent, Syed had always confounded us. With perplexing mood swings that alternated between passionate enthusiasm and abject lethargy, he was quite unpredictable. He was somebody who could stay unrealistically optimistic under the most adverse of situations and yet come across as overtly pessimistic about everyday life. He could spend countless nights perfecting the Rangoli, while tending to his grades in a manner that was almost in jest. Half seriously, he would say,

"The Rangoli challenges me more than exams do…"

Behind this intriguing exterior, lay a character that was obstinate in a quixotic sort of way. He had thought of VM as the paradise where the spirit of knowledge would be nectar for the eager mind. He had imagined being surrounded by a group of people to whom knowing and doing right was all that mattered. What he got, instead, was us; and, we found him silly.

As is the wont, the loftier one's ideals are, the greater is their tendency to shatter into pieces beyond repair. Syed was no exception. At first, he had been thrown into a fit of acute revulsion. By his own exacting standards, the criteria for success seemed too flimsy. The romantic that he was, he found it beneath himself to make any serious effort in the mad race that VM was. Gradually, revulsion turned into contempt and finally to detachment. It was only in things like Rangoli, where mettle shone above everything else, that he would come into his own.

That year, we were lagging behind in the championships and only the top honours in the Rangoli could have kept us in contention. Months before the actual event, Syed and his team of designers were already at work, sifting through the cloud of ideas for something inspired enough to be a clear winner. There were a lot of good suggestions, but Syed was not impressed – somehow they looked attractive in parts, but not as a whole. He was looking for a concept that would be a bold departure from the routine and one that would speak about our lives at VM.

When he looked at the people around him, he saw individuals quite different in their beliefs and their temperament. "Is there any similarity among us? What is it that binds us together? Is it by design?" – thus, he interrogated himself. He thought a lot about it, he kept pestering us, and one fine day, he finally had his answer. With that, the idea, too, was clear before his eyes.

⪜

The setting for *Syed's* creation was a peninsular land bordered by a vast ocean. Uneven in topography, it was the land of high mountain peaks and deep, narrow ravines. It had large swathes of wastelands and thick, impenetrable forests. But, what made it unique was its unmistakable gradient towards the ocean. It was ideal grounds for a river of irrepressible surge.

Unstoppable as the river was, as it snaked through the giant landmass on its epic journey, its efforts were augmented with streams of different hues. A little beyond its genesis, it was joined by a gushing Blue force of unbridled determination. The blueness was sky-high in its ambition and felt too much in haste. Hurriedly, it emptied itself into the river and peevishly looked on while the stream of turquoise came in from the left. Suave and restrained, the turquoise slowed down the march of the blue as a distinct pink flowed in from the right. Conscious of the surroundings, the pink was putting up a spirited fight to hold its own, when, amidst all these struggles, came in a steady yellow dignified in its quietness and blissfully oblivious of the chaos. Right before the remarkable river bent onto the plains, it was joined by a dull beige. Understated and adaptive, the beige easily blended in without a fuss.

Thus, strengthened by the different shades, the river went on. Along its course, the inevitable happened – the yellow mellowed the blue, the turquoise coloured the beige and the Pink enriched the whole. On its part, the river became a muddy brown that lay somewhere between all of them. As it neared its destination, the fertile river again split up with each stream going its own different way – though, a crucial change had taken place this time. For, the streams did leave with their own identities but also had a rich vein of brown flowing through them. The experience of mixing had obviously made them far more complete; and, this is what ultimately bound them together and prepared them for their battles with the ocean.

Needless to say, we won the championships that year. It made us ecstatic – I think it would have given a measure of satisfaction to Pandit Nehru as well.

⌐ॐ

Nehru, to me, was like a doting grandfather building colleges and factories and yet bumbling on crucial aspects of policy. Netaji, on the other hand, was like a rebellious uncle with little time for convention and reverence. And together, they made up one of the most controversial duos among those inspired souls who guided India to her freedom. One probably never got his due, while the other got more than his fair share of criticism.

The 1940s saw hypocrisy on a global scale. The world had rallied around one of the two power-hungry camps. Differences were irreconcilable and battle lines drawn, daggers unsheathed, Good was waging a crusade on evil. Or, so we were made to believe.

But, as has always been the case in history, such levels of sanctimony only served as a more convenient wrap around the much less exalted reasons of practical necessity. Apparently, the pious wanted to rid the world from the evil of an egomaniacal dictator. Apparently, they were moved by the suffering of innocent civilians. Apparently, they wanted to usher in an era of peaceful democracy. However, while performing this sacred duty, they found it convenient to side with another autocrat, no less tyrannical, and also maim the population of Hiroshima for generations to come. Incidentally, all the piety in the world did not prevent that bulwark of democracy from scoffing at the rightful representative of one-fifth of humanity as a 'naked fakir'.

If we go beyond the rhetoric of right and wrong, we find an ill-prepared world order, compelled to make dubious choices by a precarious crisis thrust upon it. When existence and freedom was at stake, tough decisions, however unpalatable, needed to be taken. I find no fault with that. Likewise, I find no fault with Netaji allying with the Germans and the Japanese to free India from the yoke of an oppressive foreign rule. Marginalized at home and faced with wartime excesses of the British, I think he was left with few other options.

However, Netaji should have known that his endeavour of trying to dislodge the British by force, was doomed from the beginning. If he had hoped that the whole of India would rise up in armed struggle and cause the mighty British Empire to implode from within, he was mistaken. With their carrot-and-stick policy, the British were more deeply entrenched and cunning in their exploitation of the vested interests plaguing the nation. He should have known that the Azad Hind Fauj – the Indian National Army – was no more than a gesture of symbolism.

History tells us that Subhas Chandra Bose, went to his martyrdom in a trail of fire and became a legend. While alive, he could not see the dream of a free India fulfilled – it was left to some of his able compatriots to make that dream a living, thriving reality; most notably Pandit Jawaharlal Nehru.

As the first prime minister of a newly independent nation, Pandit Nehru was faced with a daunting task. He had to cure the vileness of a pestilence fostered by two centuries of debilitating rule. He had to take some decisive steps to restore the glory of a fabric whose plurality was in tatters. More importantly, he had to enforce a semblance of law and order in a country that was rapidly descending into chaos.

The task was challenging and thankless. But, it had to be done and someone had to do it. Indeed, as one of the stalwarts of the freedom struggle, Nehru became the face of the Government and bore the brunt of successive generations of an ungrateful nation. Sitting today, with the benefit of hindsight, it is almost fashionable for us to tear some of his policies apart. It is probably easy for us to think that he was naïve in not being more pragmatic with the super power that was clearly in ascendance. It is probably easy for us to shoo away 'non-alignment' as misplaced idealism and denounce 'planned economy' as an example of shortsightedness. In the process, we might overlook that under the 'Bombay Plan', leading industrialists of the day exhorted and urged the Government to fill in the gaps which could not be filled by private industry alone. We might also gloss over the fact that it was largely due to Nehru's statesmanship that a newly independent nation was accorded international prestige much beyond the financial or military clout that she wielded. It is customary for us to reap the benefit of democratic institutions and yet show little regard for democracy or the person who nurtured it in its infancy. Finally, it is commonplace for every demagogue to defile the title of 'netaji' and utter the words 'Jai Hind' without even a passing thought about the values that the man stood for or the brilliant coinage of Hindu-Muslim unity that he conceived and popularized. While it is necessary to critique them and learn from their mistakes it would be a great disservice to these visionaries if we dissect their actions with little regard for the gravity of the situations they were in.

The Azad Hind Fauj, though limited in its impact as a military force, was able to ignite the imagination of millions. It was a body where man and woman, Hindu and Muslim, Punjabi and Malayali struggled towards a common goal. It was the living embodiment of unity in diversity. Similarly, institutions like VM and places like Durgapur were Nehru's experiment with plurality. Beyond the apparent objective of making careers or producing steel, there was the motive of bringing together different ways of thinking and making them strive towards a shared goal.

The 'temples of learning' and the 'white elephants', looked at from this perspective, then assume a much greater value in nation-building, than we are usually willing to concede.

The last few days at VM, came with their share of nostalgia. The day before companies came to hire us, we had the tradition of treating the hostel to a round of drinks. It was also an occasion for us to spend some quiet time together and reminisce about the past. We were huddled together in Ashish's room and sipping on rum, discreetly smuggled out of the nearby army canteen at discounted rates. Caressing the modest plastic cup, even Sundar was misty-eyed. Tomorrow we would turn a new leaf in our life. We would live different lives, some more glamorous and some less so. Tomorrow, the gulf of success would separate us. Today we could dream.

So, I dreamt...

8
THE EMPEROR AND HIS EMPIRE

The rum filled my tummy and the noxious fumes of the cigarette got into my head. Soon, I began to float, covering great distances of time and space. I finally found myself resting on a charpoy, in a room unabashedly Spartan.

I looked out of the western window where the late afternoon sun was playing hide-and-seek through the arches of the Bhati Darwaza. As it moved on its curved trajectory, it disappeared from one of the mini-arches before appearing again in another, casting a gloom of shadows on the wall behind.

Right above the window, there hung a portrait of unearthly splendor. The background was a subtle pistachio that gradually faded upwards into a soft combination of sky-blue and pale yellow. Angels swooped down from the three corners of heaven – one carrying an ornamental sword, the other an intricately decorated *chhatri* woven of fine silk and gold foil, the third holding a golden crown studded with precious emeralds, pearls and rubies. The centre of attraction was a larger-than-life figure gently stomping his authority on an olive-green globe with men and animals prostrated at his feet.

He was the Emperor, the King of the World.

Standing tall and upright, a long ceremonial staff in the right-hand and a rose in the left, he was the picture of conceit. A string of pearls bound in a saffron turban, his head was turned firmly sideways. He was wearing a long flowing robe, a tightly wound cummerbund at the waist and a tapered purple *salwar* with elaborate floral embroidery. A navel-length pearl necklace and a pair of shining arm-bands completed the set up.

Together with the finest silk and muslin that his clothes were made of and the rich array of jewels, the trappings were worth several thousands of rupees. It was usual for him. It was much more than I could hope to earn in a lifetime.

The portrait was recent, distributed free of cost by the royal palace. It came on the back of a strange *firman* decreeing us to adorn the western walls of our homes with them. I lay on the bed in awe of the kindly face surrounded by such a vulgar display of opulence. In portraits such as these the Emperor, somehow, always glanced askance as if ashamed at the night of violent orgy that marked the beginning of his reign.

Weighed down by these thoughts, I was breathing heavily when the call of the *muezzin* jolted me to my senses. I jumped out of the bed, laid down my prayer-mat on the floor, faced towards the west, knelt down and bowed to the Emperor.

Evening prayers done, I changed into my linen *salwar kameez* and headed out to Banarsi's, the local halwai. It was a hot and dry August evening – the monsoons had been unusually stingy on Lahore that year.

I swiftly zigzagged through the dark, narrow alleys carefully avoiding the filth with the deftness of a man who had taken that route many times before. There was the odd stench of a rotting animal carcass mixed with the overpowering smell of human excreta. I held my breath and quickened my pace. On reaching the blind end of the street, I did a sharp right, jogged a few steps, jumped across the overflowing drain, took another right and stopped in front of Banarsi's stall. Once there, I took deep breaths and with it the pleasing aroma of the deep-fried *samosas* went up through the nostrils into my brain. I forgot the stench.

Banarsi was famous all over Lahore for his crunchy *samosas* and sweet, crispy *jalebis*. On a hot evening like this, there was nothing better than having his *samosas* with a glass of creamy, saffron-scented *lassi*. The hot, spicy stuffing of potato singed the tongue while the cool froth of the *lassi* eased the burning. Banarsi had few parallels in the whole of *Hindustan*.

Munching on the delectable fare, I waited for the others to join.

Shod in his curved leather shoes and silk kurta, William slipped in on the vacant space beside me.

"*Salaam Waleikum!*" – he greeted in his alien accent.

"*Waleikum Salaam!* You are learning fast!" – I told him, surprised.

William was an eel of a man, smooth in his manners and seditious in his thoughts. With his shock of pale hair, deep-blue eyes, unnaturally tanned skin and extra care to blend in, he stood out. He claimed that he was from a land seven seas away, each a hundred times bigger than the Ravi. He claimed to have sailed through them in a boat as imposing as the Shahi Qila. He said that he came from a country of profiteers. He said that he was here to help. I knew he was a bag of lies.

Sadique, the Uzbek, came in late as usual. He was bilic, as always. William loved to needle him. Summoning all his fake seriousness, he suddenly asked –

"Who is an outsider?"

Before Sadique could embark on another of his energy-sapping lectures, I butted in –

"The Turks are, my folks are the rightful rulers who the Turks usurped."

Not to be left behind, Banarsi chimed in –

"Not exactly – we came in earlier than you!"

With a wry smile on his face, Bhisti the water-bearer, said –

"We were the original inhabitants that all of you drove out!"

Sadique, who had stopped frowning and was now looking at the proceedings with mild amusement, finally shook himself and sat upright. We braced ourselves for the assault.

He started…

"The 'outsider' is a shifty concept – it keeps changing from time to time. Most of us that we see around today have come to Hindustan from outside, at some point in history. Some definitely came with the idea of plunder and loot, but a lot many wanted to adopt it as their home. That they did, and over a period of time, they took to this sea of humanity like sugar takes to water. So, if we go back in time sufficiently, each one of us Turk or Pashtun, Hindu or Muslim, Aryan or Dravidian were outsiders to the ones we unsettled. That makes us equally worthy or wholly unworthy. It, then, becomes a matter of perspective. We could either look back and carry the rancour forward, or we can let bygones be bygones and work together for prosperity. I have always found the latter to be far more useful."

Though his idea of 'prosperity' was skewed, his logic was irrefutable. His way was less confrontational and much more beneficial in the long run. Expectedly, William shifted uncomfortably in his chair. For, Sadique's view made an implicit outsider of him.

Next morning, after *namaz*, I set out for work. I worked in an iron foundry together with Sadique and William. For the last few years, we had been engaged in a fruitless and seemingly endless endeavour. While, previously, we made ploughs for peasants, nowadays we did nothing but make stone-cutters and marble-chisellers. Lahore had many mouths to feed and making ploughs would have been the best use of our skills, but the Emperor was on a building spree and our job it was to tend to his whims.

When the Emperor commissioned us to make the delicate instruments that were to shape his dreams, our Ustad-ji was somewhat apprehensive. Our skills were sturdy and designed to beat intractable blocks of iron into tough farm implements. The finesse and accuracy needed for making a chisel demanded perfection of a different kind. But the Emperor's orders had to be complied with and the money was good. We took to the challenge readily.

The Ustad paid me five rupees a month – a meagre amount barely enough for my modest living. The Emperor's sudden largesse, thus, struck me as kind of an aberration. To ensure a steady supply to his building sites spread across the empire, he fixed the output from us at a minimum of 600 chisels a month. To keep us on our toes, he added a slight twist. Every month that we produced more than 600, we would get a *paisa* for each extra chisel but months when we could not meet the minimum quota, we were to be whipped.

The first few months were an anxious balancing act. We were trying to master a new art, at times with the prospect of handsome rewards and often under the shadow of the Emperor's dreaded ire. Overall, there was much more benefit in making the most of his novel rewards scheme, as it was an arrangement that came with a rider – the reward of the extra paise would go to the one who made the most chisels in a productive month while the one with the least would get all the lashings when the collective output was sub-par. This all-or-nothing tactic worked wonders and it saw each one of us trying to outdo the other and, in the process, leading to much more than the Emperor's tolerance threshold of 600. As promised, the rewards did keep pouring in, but the bulk of us still remained an unhappy lot.

William had worked at a goldsmith's, back home, and held a definite edge over us. Thus, as we were still coaxing our coarse hands to become gentler, he raced ahead. Month after month, he made much more chisels than we could count and grew richer on the Emperor's bounty. We got left behind and the disparity grew with each passing day.

I was naturally cross with the way things were progressing. I thought it unfair that the winner should get everything. I went and kept whining to Sadique. In all my grouses, Sadique saw a window of opportunity. For months now, he had been grudging William's unprecedented success and I could help him get even. I made him feel important.

He gathered around him a band of clumsy, ill-tempered losers and worked us up into a frenzy through his fiery oratory full of pompous vitriol. He swore at inequality, frothed about the virtues of class struggle and painted the dream of an unrealistic utopia where everyone shared the spoils equally and still strived for excellence. We were gullible and eager to pursue this illogical dream. In our haste, we failed to grasp basic human nature. We failed to anticipate that man, by habit, gives his best when he gets tangible value commensurate with his efforts and by removing this essential motivation, we were killing the spirit of industry and leading everyone to the lowest common denominator. We failed to understand that this kind of forced equality breeds indigence that was harmful for all. We overlooked the fact that though William became unfairly prosperous, he also saved us from the lashings that the Emperor had warned of.

Nevertheless, we opposed the current construct in true earnest. We did not go to work for days, we demonstrated in front of the royal entourage, we made ourselves a nuisance big enough for the Emperor to sit up and take note. Eventually, he came around to our view and ordered that, henceforth, the system of winner-takes-all should be abrogated in favour of a system that divided the reward equally among all of us. In keeping with this, he also reasoned that it was only fair that the punishment for not meeting the minimum quota of 600 should also be shared equally.

Months of struggle had finally borne fruit and we went home satisfied.

Under the inequitable system, William had, on an average, made extra twenty paise every month – a princely sum that had egged all of us to outdo him. Under the current system of equitable distribution, those twenty paise split equally among all 500 of us, counted for nothing. It did not seem worth all the pain. We began doing just enough to avoid the Emperor's wrath. Gradually, our monthly output started slipping till we had difficulty in keeping up to the minimum standards. Impatient with our inconsistency, the Emperor ultimately raised the bar a notch, to 610 a month. But, by that time, we had forgotten our trade to such an extent that lashings became inevitable.

This had been the story for all of last year. We had been led astray and at the end of every month as we lined up to receive the customary caning, we would be jolted into our senses for a brief, painful period. As the vicious lash left a bloody streak on our backs, we would take comfort in the knowledge that we were, after all, in equal misery.

Only on unusually perceptive moments, as I lay alone on my bed, I repented the futility of it all. Sadique had the unique gift of organizing mass movements. If only he had put it to better use! I wondered what would have happened if, instead of fighting over how to go about making chisels, he had got us together to pose more pertinent questions to the Emperor. Could we have got his priorities rectified? Would we have been able to get his focus away from the chisel onto the plough?

⁓

Although upset to start with, William reconciled himself to the unimaginativeness around him. As far as he was concerned, the Hindustanis could bicker into inconsequence – it was all the better, his time would come sooner than anticipated. As a boy, his imagination had been fired by the incredible tale of the Venetian who embarked on one of the most historic journeys of the medieval world. As he carried the phial of holy water from Jerusalem to Xanadu, he spoke of exotic and remote lands full of untold riches. Though a fair bit of it was exaggeration, it is easy to comprehend why William, coming from an unremarkably tiny island off the coast of a continent in perpetual strife, would have found the story promising enough. Whether it was the dearth of resources at home, the petty quarrels in his immediate vicinity, the lure of the lucre or the spirit of inquiry, the canvass of his dreams were much more grand than what the insignificant island could ever hope to offer. He had global domination in his restive mind and with the perfection of the ocean-faring ship the future was his for the taking. He set sail.

In stark contrast, the Emperor, in his delusion of being the King of the World, had shut his doors to it. He was convinced of his supremacy and did not feel the urge to recognize that which lay beyond the confines of Hindustan. In fact, the only envoys that he ever sent were to Isfahan in Persia and even there, he was like a big brother chiding a young upstart. Condescending as he was, he often reserved the most patronizing of his haughtiness for William and his ilk. Decked in his glittering best, he would strut like a peacock in front of them and become almost ecstatic seeing the look of awe in their eyes. Self-absorbed, he would often miss the foxy slyness and the nerves of steel behind that look of amazement. The Emperor, thus blinded by his wealth, had tricked himself into a laxness so unusual to his kind. For, was it not one of his blood that had made the journey of the Venetian possible? Was it not the same vitality that now made a William had, in the past, brought another of his own to Hindustan?

Firmly moored in the present as he was, the Emperor ignored the lessons of the past and provided precious little for the future. If he had been a little more clairvoyant, he would have seen the writing on the wall clearly. He would have looked around himself and understood that knowledge was power in the world of tomorrow. If he had understood that, he would have been the catalyst in making his subjects wiser. If he wanted his future generations to prosper, he would probably have built a far greater number of institutions that took learning to the common man.

He failed to do that and unfortunately, so engrossed was I with my daily battles with food, clothing & shelter and so unshakeable was my belief in the Emperor's pretence, that I too misread William.

The Emperor had definitely shunned the world, but it was not as if there were no outsiders in his court. For, the enormous wealth that his forefathers had accumulated and which he was so gaily throwing away attracted a lot of people looking to make a quick buck. Thus, poets, architects and astrologers homed in from all corners of the world to massage his ego and feed on his morsels. They composed elaborate panegyrics, built magnificent monuments and made up obscure constellations – all confirming his greatness. Oblivious to the damage, they played along in his belief that he was the chosen one with a divine right over the world for eternity. Somewhere in the midst of this grand drama, the Emperor, his viziers and the coterie of talent in his court, forgot about me.

And that was their undoing.

～

The next evening we were at Banarsi's when I noticed a mouse in an erratic dance of death. It rushed out from behind the wooden pole and scurried around aimlessly for a while. It then went towards the hot oven, stopped midway, quickly retraced its steps back to the pole, made a valiant effort to climb it and fell off. Bruised and tired, it wanted to outrun the terrible agony it was in. Pausing for a brief moment at the foot of the pole, it made one last headlong dash towards the side. On reaching the wall, it started banging its head with a ferocious urgency till the insides of its rodent brain burst out and lay splattered, lifeless on the ground. In the last few moments of its wretched life, it must have cursed bitterly the futile torment that its existence was.

The scourge of the plague was upon us! Nobody, not even the mighty Emperor was safe from the epidemic. Our only chance lay in mass exodus.

"Let's get away from here!" – I exclaimed.

"God! I will run away to the forest!" – despaired Banarsi.

"I will go back to Fergana. My future lies in the Steppes. There's nothing left for me here" – remarked Sadique, fatalistically.

"Why not go to Agra?" – William seemed visibly excited.

Banarsi had a flourishing business to get back to, Sadique had future revolutions to foment and William just had new lands to discover. I was in a far deeper mess.

I heard them all. Certainly, Lahore with its frontier placement was a strategic location, but was definitely far off from the current seat of action. In times of territorial expansion, it had served its usefulness as a secure bastion of the empire. However, the security threat from the north-west had been quelled to a great extent and the Emperor was now focused on consolidation and subjugation of the still unconquered lands to the south. Thus, in an effort to manage the vast lands under him better and direct new campaigns in the Deccan, he had shifted base to Agra. As the imperial capital, *Agra* commanded much better favour from the Emperor these days. With its newer citadel, graced by the person of the Emperor himself, Agra was as much the playground for his grandiose dreams as the nerve-centre of the empire. And, given the imminence of the plague and my destitution in Lahore, *Agra* represented a new beginning. If I had the means of the Emperor I would have fled, lock stock and barrel, to the cooler climes of Kashmir. But Agra was good enough – maybe by virtue of being closer, some of the Emperor's good fortune will rub onto me, maybe I could make a life by feeding off his magnanimity.

"To Agra!", I declared, vaguely aware of the troublesome travel it entailed. There was hardly any time left, prudence said that we leave as soon as possible.

Lahore to Agra was a few kos less than 200, slightly over 400 miles according to William. It amounted to a tough month's journey on the *Badshahi Sadak*, the Royal Road that connected the eastern and north-western extremities of the empire. Cutting across lands semi-arid as well as incredibly fertile, it was the life-blood of the nation serving as a conduit for travelers, merchants and often, the imperial armies. For the most part, it ran in a rough south-easterly fashion to Agra, crossing great rivers and carefully avoiding the deserts of the Rajputana. Along the way, one went through important cities, nondescript villages and huge tracts of the lawless and bandit infested countryside. To provide succour to the tired, the entire route was dotted by a string of caravanserais that the nobility had built on the Emperor's orders. Many a merchant and traveler had made their fortune on the road – what was essential was a little bit of luck, lots of street-smartness and some planning to avoid the dangers it posed. Traveling in a group greatly increased the chances of getting to the destination safe and sound.

Asking around, we learnt that a caravan presently camped at Sarai Shahu-Garhi on the banks of the Ravi, was due for Agra the day after. Early next morning we went to inspect the noisy crowd of camels, oxen and carts laden with men and merchandise. Mostly a rag-tag bunch, there were the few fortunate ones, with silken robes, riding palanquins and proudly showing-off the majestic Arabian steeds at their disposal. They were almost all merchants bound for the bustling market and the imperial mint at *Agra*. Well guarded by a private militia, it seemed a safe enough option for a couple of men uninitiated to the unpredictability of the terrain and temperament of the Hindu heartland.

Approaching a dirty, sorry looking face I asked, "Bhai, the two of us want to go to Agra. Can we join you?"

"Go ask the *Bakshi*" – he spat at us.

The *Bakshi* was the captain of the caravan. As the in-charge of the group, it was he who selected the halts, decided when it was time to move, arranged for the security and negotiated with the customs officials, enroute. His duty was to see the caravan safely till the end. It was an ancient trade that he had learnt from his father and the importance of his being was not lost on him. Without his consent, we would not be allowed into the group.

Summoning all the reverence I could, I pleaded – "*Janab*, we are two unfortunate souls eager to seek the blessings of the Emperor. *Inshallah*, with your help, our wish would be granted. Will you take us along with you?"

"*Bismillahi Rahamanir Raheem*! I am but a mere servant guiding the faithful on their way. If you are resolute enough, who am I to go against *Allah's* wishes?" – he looked down with pompous humility. "You have to get your own ox and cart, else you walk. Ten rupees apiece, is all I need for my services," he added as an afterthought.

Ten rupees was a princely sum for either of us and after parting with that, we could hardly afford either a cart or an ox. Traveling by foot was daunting, but our callous soles were accustomed to a lot of inconvenience and the thought of covering 400 miles on foot was not that discouraging. We agreed to his terms and paid him.

Thus settling with the *Bakshi*, I went back to spend the remainder of my last day at home. There were the customary farewells to bid, the wishful promises of meeting again to make and the pain of severing deep-rooted bonds to nurse. I went to Banarsi and hugged him tightly. Sadique was present as well. We reminded each other of the good days that we had seen together and prayed that we see much better days ahead. I surveyed the benches where we had spent many an evening sharing jokes or palace gossip. With a long look, I gathered all the memories and locked them in an unreachable corner of my mind and threw the key away. I then went back to my *charpoy* and slept like a log.

At dawn, the next day, I woke up and set off into the unknown. Save a few provisions and the *Pir Baba's* amulet, I had only my hopes for comfort. I was traveling light. So was William – he was carrying his dreams along. We crossed the Ravi and came to the head of the camp. Already bustling with activity, man and beast was waiting for the *Bakshi* to signal the start.

For the last time, I looked back, over my shoulder, to what I was leaving behind. As I strained my eyes, I could faintly make out the dim outline of my *mohalla* through the columns of smoke rising from the surrounding neighbourhoods. All of a sudden, I was seized with a strange impulse. In a brief, ambivalent moment I thought of re-considering my decision. My family had come to Lahore from Ghazni almost three centuries ago. Our origins were shrouded in the hoary past and Lahore was the only place I called home. To desert the city I loved so much, to uproot myself from the alleyways that I knew like the back of my hand and submit myself to fate's mercy was not an easy decision. For a moment, I thought that let the plague be – why need I abandon my *watan* – my home? But the urge to live was overwhelming, that I quickly admonished myself at my rashness. Men like me could hardly afford to have very strong preferences. We were like feather in a heavy wind – blown around by the storm of circumstances. Good or bad, we had always been swayed by the quirks of those who wielded power and the fortune that they granted us. Where persecution had forced my people to make the journey to Lahore, the prospect of death by disease was again pushing me on the move. Once more, it made me a man without a land.

A sinking hollowness overcame me as I slowly hardened myself.

With changing times, Lahore too had seen her fortune wax and wane. She had outlived dynasties and I was sure that she would find the strength to rise up from the ashes. In a different day and a different age, she would once again be the home of culture and civilization. I might not be around, but a part of me would return to witness her splendour. I wished her all the best for the storm ahead and trudged on, determined not to look back.

At the precise time that the astrologers had marked most auspicious to embark on a journey of this magnitude, the *Bakshi* gave the call to start. Almost immediately, a shiver ran through the column as if suddenly stretched to attention with a sharp crack of the whip. Itchy camels bent their legs at the knees and swept forward, anxious oxen tugged at their carts and with '*Allahu Akbar*' on my lips I took my first tentative step.

We went in files of 8 to 10, a rigid hierarchy on the move. The *Bakshi* rode at the forefront with a detachment of armed guards shadowing him. Immediately after him came the palanquin bearers carrying their silken masters with their bullion-laden camel-carts and their prize horses following closely behind. Next were the lesser merchants with bullock carts full of ordinary wares. William, I and numerous other foot travelers made up the rear. We slackened the pace of the group and were so placed as to be the last to reach every *sarai*, after the others had negotiated for the best available rooms.

The *Badshahi Sadak* was quite unlike anything I had seen before. A world apart from the narrow and crooked streets of the *mohalla*, it was clean, broad and straight for as far as I could see. The surface was of baked mud and we were a mass of hooves and hide leaving behind a cloud of dust in our wake. *Bhistis* carrying leather-pouches sprinkled water taming the dust intermittently. Rows of mulberry trees, planted on either side, arched over the road making a natural passageway of cool shade for our ease. Even with the scant rains, the trees were green and thick with leaves, flowers and fruits in full bloom. Their soft aroma jostled with the stench of dung and sweat of the moving caravan.

Navigating the highway was an entirely new experience. The narrow streets of my *mohalla* were claustrophobic. I had negotiated them from memory, counting my steps to each turn I wanted to make, each corner I wanted to avoid and each drain that I had to jump over. In a sense, it was a sequential enactment of steps aided by external cues. Rarely had I felt the need of mapping out more than my immediate few paces, with the high walls of the city obstructing my view to an extent that knowing what lay beyond my line of sight was wholly impractical. The highway was different – with an abundance of open spaces and an unimpeded view of the horizon, I saw things and adjusted myself long before I was physically near them. I felt uniquely empowered. We were buoyant and made decent progress.

Our first stop on the route was at Sarai Khan-i-Khanan beside a large manmade reservoir of water, the Raja Taal. It was a medium sized inn with a modest Buland Darwaza, the triumphant arch that led to an open courtyard with rooms at the periphery. By the time we reached, all the rooms had been taken and we had to make space for ourselves in the courtyard between the camels and the oxen. I was hardly bothered – the night was cool, the sky was clear and shone brilliantly.

I was tired and hungry and ran through the naan and kebab in a matter of minutes. Thirsty, I headed out to the taal and filled myself with a hearty drink from its sweet, dark waters. Once satisfied, I made a dash to reclaim my prime position in the courtyard.

I laid face up on the flat, hard surface resting my head against the inside of my palm and looked up. A pitch-black moonless night, with nature at her prodigal best, greeted me whole-heartedly. Countless stars were carelessly strewn on the blackness like gems and emeralds embroidered on a rich noblewoman's robe. The stars were not all the same. Some dazzled with the vigour of youth while others sobered from the reflected glow of a past more illustrious. In form and shape, they were tiny specks of fire unevenly scattered over the fabric of the robe. Mischievous and alluring, the robe was an expansive veil over the ethereal beauty of paradise. The haphazardness of the arrangement seduced me with the symmetry that it was masking.

From where I lay, the grandness was within grasp. I reached up, connected the dots and started sketching mythical shapes and figures on the magnificent canvass that nature spread out in front of me. I drew a unicorn gracefully stretching its horns upwards, a centaur flinging a giant arrow from its larger-than-life bow, a majestic sphinx lying on its belly with the paws outstretched – I went on. Ever so often, a runaway streak of light darted in from the corner and bumped against my creation causing me to start all over again. I drew and felt sorry for the Emperor. Would he, from his fortified ramparts, be privy to a grandeur of this scale? Could he, harried by the care of throne and crown, have the luxury of an indulgence such as this? I was really blessed, I thought.

At some point, I fell asleep.

I woke up to a commotion in front of the *Bakshi's* room. The sun was just about peeking over the eastern sky and the *Bakshi* was engaged in a verbal duel with the astrologer traveling with us. It transpired that he had misread the charts earlier and in a moment of remarkable clarity, that only a clear sky could engender, the act of omission had dawned upon him. His new calculations said that we should prolong our stay at the sarai by three days, at the least. The uncharacteristic smile on the dour inn-keeper's face hinted at the possibility of a commission as well, but the *Bakshi* was not amused. He dared not enrage his stars by going against the certainties of fortune. It was evident that we had to kill time.

We were destined to wait, but William had a better idea. He had heard of a new phenomenon in the town of Amritsar that he was eager to explore. It would be good use of the fortuitous delay, he felt. I was happy to tag along.

With a rough map at the back of our minds, William and I set off. Amritsar lay off-track, slightly to the north-east. It was a rebellious place where the writ of the Emperor was hardly, if ever, the last word. The Emperor, on the other hand, spared no trick to discredit its symbolism and that of its people. There was no proper road, yet, that connected it to the outside world. To other parts of the empire, it was made to be a land of unusual villainy.

Our inquisitiveness took us through dense fields of wheat and paddy. The rains, though late in coming, was no more than a minor blip against the magic of a land blessed by five mineral-rich rivers. Everywhere I looked, I saw a cover of green – the fruit of a rare mixture of bounty and uncompromising toil. The entire landscape was partitioned into holdings square in shape and bordered by bunds of mud. Aside from marking out territory, the bunds were essential in keeping the crops partly submerged and fully nourished. Within them sturdy farmers knee-deep in water tilled their lands. Shouting encouragement to the bullocks pulling the ploughs, they went about their task with customary efficiency. Confident and self-assured, they did not appear to be at the mercy of nature.

Balancing precariously on the bunds and often stopping to ask directions, we made a slow but steady progress. We crossed the farmers and came upon a line of women en route to the village pond. They were on their way to the daily ritual of bathing, washing and collecting water for the kitchen. While the men nurtured the crops, they nurtured the homes. Our presence sent a flutter of shyness. Pulling the *duppatta-s* over their faces they held it in place by the corner of their mouths, firmly discouraging the prying look in our eyes.

"Which way to Amritsar?" – I enquired.

In between giggles, the woman at the front replied, "How would I know? I have never been to Amritsar. But yes, my grandfather went there once, just after the Great Famine. Walking from the Gurudwara into the new sun he had reached by the time the sun was behind him while his shadow walked a few steps ahead. You should take the same road."

Leaving them to stare incredulously at us, we went in search of that elusive Gurudwara. It was not far from where we stood. Reaching there, we continued in the direction she pointed. As the day progressed, we went from field to village and back to field again. By the fag end of the afternoon, we were on the outskirts of Amritsar.

The phenomenon that had so attracted *William* was a muted act of defiance being played out in front of a deathly pale crowd. Despite the extreme discontentment, the crowd was strangely silent. This vacuum of noise sucked us from the outskirts of the city in front of a park quite different than the usual. The park was set in a natural depression surrounded by high walls. Entry and exit was through a narrow opening in the corner, barely enough for either William or me to just squeeze in sideways. We went in one at a time, bending slightly to avoid hitting the roof of the entrance and climbed down the mud steps into the park.

We were greeted by rows of haggard faces squatting in reverent silence around a central dais hastily erected out of bamboo and wood. On the dais sat an ordinary peasant, an unlikely hero of the gathered mass. He was not from the nobility and looked ill-supplied with resources, but the degree of adulation that he commanded was evident to all. With dark circles around his sunken, hollow eyes he was protagonist of a remarkable movement against the Emperor. A life full of hunger, pain, death, disease and poverty was a bane for the average Hindustani. The blame, for all of that, he laid squarely on the Emperor's inaction. He was campaigning to wake the Emperor up from his slumber – he wanted him to act in our interest. Fed up of the Emperor's policies, he had gone unfed for the last ten days. He was, now, hungry for response.

William and I took up a vantage position on one side of the crowd. It was a hot and humid evening and the oppressive heat only served to increase the bitterness. Even the well at the eastern corner had dried up causing dissatisfaction to run higher. The peasant and his followers had been sulking like schoolboys in the fantastic hope that the Emperor, steeped as he was in his arrogance, could be moved into giving them a patient hearing. Long exploited by *zamindars* who exacted harsh taxes, *rahadars* who levied false duties and *mansabdars* who did not police, they had turned to the Emperor, the *Refuge of the World*, as a last resort. Alas! The Emperor was much too preoccupied with his dreams to even take notice. He, who routinely appropriated our devotion to the crown, had little time for the man on the street. Moreover, the peasant had committed a cardinal sin – he had dared to challenge the inviolable notions of peace, security and unquestioned obedience. He had dug his own grave.

Ever since he had pitched tent on a fateful August morning, the peasant had set in motion a chain of events. Cronies and officials, habitually derelict in their duties, had suddenly become hyper-efficient. They had responded with hectic, behind the scenes politicking to break up determined resistance. They had tugged and scratched at different interest groups in the crowd trying to bribe some, browbeat others and undermine everyone. They had expended a lot of energy in misguided endeavours without ever pausing to have an open and sincere dialogue. Where a genuine admission of failure could have sowed the seeds of a new, constructive era, their games of one-upmanship further ossified the distrust.

Increasingly desperate and disillusioned, the peasant finally broke his vow of silence at the dead of night. Raising his pitch, he exhorted his passionate followers. He cried –

"The hour of reckoning is near. It's do or die from now on!"

Ultimately, this was the provocation that everyone was waiting for.

Relentless campaigning had taken its toll on the weary crowd and we were snatching a few precious moments of sleep when an angry grunt woke me up in the wee hours of the morning. Startled, I peeked out through the narrow entrance of the park and saw a wall of elephants charging towards us. Incited by their *mahouts* they had the look of murder in their beastly eyes. The over-zealous governor of the Punjab was keen to ingratiate himself with the Emperor. And, hearing of the open call for insubordination, he had seized his opportunity. Overnight, he had amassed a sizeable portion of his elephant battalion and let loose the full force of imperial might upon us. The impertinent needed to be taught a lesson – the opposition had to be trampled at any cost.

Confused and shocked, we sat transfixed for a moment. And then we ran. Babies, their sleep abruptly broken, started wailing. Mothers held them to their bosoms and ran for the wall. We fled towards the wall. The wall was very steep and very slippery – scaling it was no mean task. The hapless among us began banging their heads on it in sheer frustration. But William and I had not run away from plague to meet our ends under the lumbering tuskers of the empire. With death tantalizingly close, we put in all we could and finally jumped over the wall. Even on the other side, we did not stop running. We ran all the way back to the *sarai* and finally stopped once safely inside its relative anonymity. Exhausted and drained, I collapsed on the ground and slept like a log.

I had had a first-hand brush with imperial authority and had lived to tell the tale. I was lucky, but many were not – I shuddered to think of their plight. However, this rather unpleasant incident had done a world of good to my belief. For the first time I felt that I could reach Agra and see the Emperor in person. In one sweep, he had lowered himself from the larger than life image that I had bowed down to in my Lahore home. In his immature act of vengeance, he seemed like a petty chief.

We resumed our journey the next morning. Already delayed by a few days, the *Bakshi* was in no mood to relax. He pressed us on, at a punishing pace, towards the *sarai* of Sultanpur Lodhi near the town of Kapurthala. Dirty and dying of thirst, he only allowed us a brief respite at the Goindwal Baoli on the banks of the Beas. I had been traveling over the dusty plains since morning and all that my tired mind wanted was water. Situated under the cool shade of a huge banyan tree, the octagonal well of the *baoli* was like a magnet. I doubled down its spacious stairway into the pool of water below. In my hurry, I barely noticed the flight of eighty-four steps that took me deep beneath the ground. Splashing my heat-ravaged face with the kind, fresh water of the pool, I was profuse in my gratefulness to the individual who had built it for me.

The individual in question was an influential farmer who lived a century ago. The recent incident at Amritsar was hardly an aberration – it was but the latest flare-up in a long history of confrontation. Ever since an unjust execution, the empire was in an uneasy truce with the peasants of the Punjab, the land of the five rivers and the granary of Hindustan. Proud and confident of their abilities, the *Punjabi* peasantry had found the demands of caste and ceremony an unnecessary overhead. To add to this confusion, the ideological clash between monotheism and polytheism, often scarring their fertile homeland and compelled them to think differently. In this general environment of religious strife, there arose a group of men professing a simple way of living with equality at its core. Their remarkable clarity of thought, considerable powers of persuasion and personal probity appealed to the rank and file of the Punjab. Attracted by this novel philosophy that determined one's place in society by deeds and not by birth, they joined the new order en masse. And, that placed them in direct conflict with the empire. For, the Punjab was no ordinary province. It controlled the movement of foodgrain and was also a strategic buffer against invading armies from the north west. Further, the empire felt threatened by the unification of resourceful people under the banner of faith. It was a vocal group that could challenge the authority of the Emperor. With a measure of haste, the Emperor reacted in the time-tested manner of all monarchs – under the pretext of unity, he decided to crush the movement with brute force.

On hindsight, that was a gross error of judgment. It only hardened the resolve of the Punjabis and made dangerous rebels out of a fiercely belligerent people. Years of nominal gestures and several conciliatory measures notwithstanding, the tension still simmered under the outward garb of stability. Only on days like the one at Amritsar did the unhealed wounds of the past become apparent to one and all.

In fact, the Emperor, impervious as he was to logic and reason, had made a habit of getting embroiled in one costly stalemate or the other.

The Isfahanis, one of the handful of dynasties fortunate enough to merit notice from the Emperor, were up to their own mischief. Lacking in human and financial resources as well as wary of a frontal assault, they plotted to wear him down. Disheartened by reversals in a few skirmishes in Kabul, they simply found it beneficial to wage a proxy war in the *Deccan*. The Emperor, suffering from the myth of invincibility, was easily drawn into the sticky mess of Deccani politics. The sultanates of Bijapur and Golconda were to the extreme south of the sub-continent. The geography of the region had kept them immune from the monarchy at Agra and over-stretching of supply lines, as also local resilience with material support from Isfahan, had made a final solution, elusive. Despite several bloody campaigns, the Deccan still remained an unresolved question.

As always, the common man had been the casualty in this power game. Loss of life and property, on either side, had been huge. More harmful had been the wasting of the countryside with each of the armies taking turns in pillaging the villages that lay in the way.

For me, an ordinary traveler on the road, the whole issue was difficult to comprehend. Did the Emperor not have enough territories under his control to bother about the Deccan? How many more diamonds could the mines of Deccan add to his treasury? Were they worth the astronomical waste that the conquest was proving to be? By allowing himself to obsess with it, was he not neglecting other aspects of statecraft? Could regions and people be 'mainstreamed' by force alone? How much more important was prejudice-free cultural assimilation? Even if he were able to win over by force, would he be able to hold on to it in the long run? What was Isfahan gaining from our suffering? Was it not just a matter of letting go of one's ego?

These were questions that clouded my mind as I took a short nap on the steps of the *Goindwal Baoli*. Soon, the *Bakshi* poked my ribs and woke me up from my reverie. Jolted back to reality, I marched on to Sarai Sultanpur Lodhi.

It was drizzling when we could finally make out the outline of the *sarai*. In the darkness, the string of lights on its imposing *Buland Darwaza* was like a beacon of hope for the harried traveler. We quickened our pace and reached the gate just as the rain was increasing in intensity. I jostled through the crowd, making my way to the nearest dry corner of the hallway. Spreading my cotton mat, I sank onto the ground sleeping the lengthy motionless sleep of a dead tired man.

I woke up quite late, the next morning. We were to stay in the *sarai* for that day and I was in little hurry – I went on a leisurely stroll of the place. It was certainly one of the biggest *sarais* that I had ever seen. The majestic arch of the gate and the fortified walls enclosed a massive place that boasted of a large inn with hundreds of rooms, a small mosque on one side and a bustling bazaar at the centre. The rooms of the inn were arranged in multiple floors around the central open courtyard. They were of varying sizes – the *Bakshi* occupied the airiest one on the topmost floor while the lesser merchants huddled with their wares in one of the smaller ground floor rooms.

Bandits were always a threat in wayside locations such as these and no effort had been spared to discourage them. As if the thick outer walls were not enough, tall watch towers at each corner, constantly manned by sentries, served to reinforce the sense of peace and security within. To add to it, there was the forbidding plaque at the entrance:

In the name of the Emperor, the Merciful

You must ensure that traders can rest without fear of harm and trade their goods without worry. Maintaining the peace and prosperity of the Empire is your duty. If you are found in violation of this decree, you will be pursued even to the farthest corners of hell.

Stern as it was, the import of the plaque was clearer to me as the day progressed. The *sarai* with its formidable fifteen-metre walls and armed sentries still needed to remind the passersby of the legitimacy of the empire. For, far from the urban power-centres, the countryside was still under the iron grip of laws and figures that had remained unchanged for generations and, in an atmosphere like this, deference to imperial rule was fickle at best. Rulers came and went, but the lot of the villages had remained largely untouched for over a millennium. The Emperor, pragmatic in his dealings and obsessed with the longevity of his reign, thought it prudent to not meddle in the affairs of the village as long as his sources of revenue were intact. However, this calculated latitude often encouraged the more ambitious village chiefs to act beyond their loosely prescribed limits of discretion and try out their luck at a larger slice of the revenue pie. And that gave rise to the banditry. Remarkably, the standoffish Emperor could be unusually vigorous when his treasury was at stake. As if to drive the message deep into the hinterlands of Hindustan, the impregnable *sarai* and the stern plaque were symbolic reminders of the brutal force backing up the empire. They were designed specifically as to leave no doubt about who the boss really was and the degree of retribution that he could demand. For thousands of villages and millions of villagers, that was the only way the Emperor ever touched their lives.

I was just getting off my noon prayers when the mass of villagers started trickling in. They had set off from their homes in the morning and trekked long distances to reach the *sarai*. Once at the bazaar, they took up their favoured positions and began arranging their wares. Pulses, cereals, livestock, provisions for cooking, timbre for fire and other items useful for the itinerant were neatly arranged in the various stalls. Apart from products of daily use, there were the occasional trinkets that one could take as a gift to the beloved and miniature wooden toys to bring a smile on the face of the child left behind at home.

William was especially attracted by a pair of dolls that one of the villagers had spread out on the ground. The dolls were a farmer couple attired in the traditional dress of the *bhangra*, the harvest dance. They wore brightly coloured *kurtas* at the top and *lungis* at the waist. Over the *kurta*, each had a half-sleeved breast jacket hemmed by strips of shining fabric. Small handkerchiefs clasped in their hands, an elaborate turban on the man and a long *chunni* on the woman completed the get-up.

Inspecting the dolls, *William* asked, "How much for these?"

"One *anna, sahib*", replied the vendor.

"That's too much! I won't pay more than a paisa!", retorted William, with feigned surprise.

"*Sahib,* you are fortunate, I am not. I have six mouths to feed. I work hard day and night on the fields while my wife makes these dolls. Once every seven days I come here to sell my toys so that I can take away some food for my family. One paisa is not even enough to cover my expenses of coming here. Please sahib, have some mercy on me!" – pleaded the vendor with the necessary dramatization.

"Ok! I will give two paise, nothing more than that!", said William and started to walk away.

"Two paise will just meet the cost. But, you are the first customer of the day and I can make an exception for you. Thank you sahib! God will bless you for helping out a poor soul", replied the vendor as he wrapped the dolls in a piece of paper and handed it over to William in the same manner that he had done to five other customers that day.

I moved around aimlessly haggling with the stall-owners and quoting ridiculously low prices. After a while, they realized that I did not intend to buy anything and stopped attending to me. I got bored and went back to my mat and the shady corner of the hallway. The *Bakshi* had said that Sultanpur Lodhi would be a temporary reprieve for the days ahead and I wanted to make the most of the rest that we got. Early next morning we moved on.

The *Bakshi* said that the next phase of our journey was the most crucial. According to him, it often proved to be the deciding factor between success and failure. When we had started from Lahore, we all were under the impetus of enthusiasm. Some were in a hurry to leave the past behind while others eagerly awaited the future. But, for the majority of us, the novelty of being on the road, seeing new lands and getting new experiences was a big enough pull. It was a pull that had us steer through the hardships of travel with a cheerful disposition. It was a pull that had made the *Bakshi's* exacting demands of pace seem quite natural. However, we had been traveling for close to two weeks now and the novelty factor had worn down. It was that period of the journey when, as the *Bakshi* said, the destination seemed too far and the challenge too daunting. He felt it absolutely critical that we dispel all notions of resignation and remain focused on the road.

The *Bakshi's* words were prophetic as soon enough I found myself engulfed by similar doubts.

We crossed the Sutlej near Phillaur, but strangely it did not evoke the kind of emotions that the Ravi always did. The breeze was not as refreshing, the river did not seem as big, the water tasted far less sweet. I had been away from home for long and each step was beginning to feel like a drag. Leaving Lahore was inevitable but was faraway Agra the right choice? Could I even make it there on my feet?

The next few days were a pitched battle between heart and mind and the *Bakshi* occasionally trooping in with his usual words of encouragement. From Phillaur we went to Ludhiana, then to Sirhind and from there to Ambala. We took several twists and turns while the landscape turned gradually from flat green fields to bushy undergrowth before beginning to fade into a dusty, semi-arid brown.

We halted at various *sarais* along the way and went through different villages and towns that increasingly looked a replica of the rest. Every single bone creaked in agony, every muscle was up in arms at the demands I made on myself. Against this overwhelming fatigue, even a seasoned traveler like William found it hard to keep up the tempo. But the *Bakshi* was in no mood to compromise – he made us do Ambala to Karnal in one single day. Spending the night there, we raced on.

We fought through the fateful plains of Panipat and waved over the ups and downs of Sonipat. Egged on by the *Bakshi* and held together by the guilt of the deserter I hung on, dangerously close to the limits of my physical ability. Till, one weary evening, shoulders drooping, the Yamuna shone the dull red of the tired sun.

We were approaching the provincial headquarters of *Dilli*.

It was late when we finally trooped into the *Arab Sarai*, built on a piece of land considered eternally sacred. The shrine of Hazrat Nizamuddin lay at a stone's throw showering divine blessings on all who cared to stop by. The long departed Saint's philosophy on the union of Man with God through purification of the inner self had exerted a powerful influence on the local populace. This purification, as he envisaged, lay not in ritualistic doctrine but in loving the Maker and serving His Creations. Thus, shorn of the strictures of faith, the path that he professed was at once simple and inclusive. In time, this appealing message of love, music and mysticism had spread much beyond the confines of *Dilli* and even now, centuries after his death, he drew a wide array of followers cutting across class and religion. The royal mausoleum adjoining the *sarai*, so situated as to seek the Saint's intervention in the afterlife, was a testament to the regard that people still had for his mystic prowess.

Unlike the shrine whose attractiveness lay undiminished through the vicissitudes of time, the *Dilli* that we stepped into was like an aging courtesan still smarting from the decline of fortunes. Particularly woeful were the ruins around the city that spoke of a rich, historic past which had now all but withered away. For, the *Dilli* that was now a mere provincial town had, till not far ago, been the city of kings. Its geo-strategic and historical importance meant that it had always been the city to conquer for anybody wanting to stake a legitimate claim over Hindustan. Unfortunately, this significance also meant that it had often been an unwilling pawn in many an unsavoury power game. Throughout history, a hodge podge of rulers and dynasties had fought over the city and its riches. As is the wont, with every new ruler came in a period of extraordinary affluence followed by the inevitable decline and ultimate demise at the hands of a more vigorous usurper. Each ruler, during his heyday, had adorned the city with wonderful monuments and other riches, only for them to languish under the changed priorities of the new king.

The heap of ruins, though a more visible reminder of the cyclical fortune that the city had witnessed, was in no way more impacted than the inhabitants themselves. Scarred by fate, as they were, I found the Dilliwala a very god-fearing person. As if afraid to be caught on the wrong side of the new invader round the corner, he tended to keep his cards close to his chest, living in the present with only a mournful look at the past and a very real apprehension of the future. For a city privy to political machinations of every kind, the Dilliwala, appeared unusually apolitical and in an absolute hurry to forget the past.

However, looks, as I later found out, could be quite deceptive. For, though it was true that the average Dilliwala was forever short of resources and always gingerly in tending to his roots, he had devised other innovative, albeit less conspicuous, ways of keeping the past alive. While he was apathetic towards monuments and documented history, he was equally enthusiastic about oral tradition. For him, the immortality of the past lay not in preserving architecture and chronicles, but in keeping history alive through anecdotes passed on from the parent to the child. And, over a period of time, these anecdotes got crystallized into quaint customs, odd superstitions and indisputable truisms that, if investigated today, seem like traces of the past mutilated but seamlessly intertwined with the mundane everyday life of the present. By virtue of this richness of legends and his strong tribal affiliations, the Dilliwala was like a living and breathing remnant of the long and chequered history that the city had seen. Unfortunately for him and inexplicably for outsiders, the inheritance of such a rich legacy did make him a bit reckless as to its value. In this, he was quite similar to how *Hindustanis* had generally behaved over the ages.

Of all the themes recurrent among the townsfolk, I found one particularly intriguing. Apparently, legend had it that Dilli was a city with a jinx. It was a jinx that attracted plunderers and invaders alike. It was a jinx that so charmed them that they often forgot to plunder and decided to settle down in this city. Ironically, this also led to their downfall. For, according to the Jinx, anyone who decided to re-build the city of *Dilli* ultimately paid with his own destruction. The simplicity and significance of this tale was especially pertinent, given the rumours afoot that the Emperor was considering shifting his capital from Agra to Dilli.

⟶

I was already fed-up with the traveling when we reached Dilli. After a longish halt there, I was even more tempted to give up the idea of going to Agra. To add to this, was the news that the *jagirdar* of Palwal, a roadside village, had a family wedding due to which he had pitched a tent on a tract of the *Badshahi Sadak*, effectively cutting out all to and fro traffic on the road. The celebration had been going on for a few days now and was expected to continue till the next fortnight.It meant that we either waited at Dilli or found some alternate route.

The *jagirdar* of Palwal, in reality an unranked busybody of the Empire, considered himself a very important person. In fact, he took self-importance to such an extreme that inconveniencing the common man was just collateral damage. When he was not pitching a tent on the road, he was usually obstructing traffic by ensuring that his entourage had the right of way. He always traveled in style, stayed at the best of rooms, did not bother about customs and duties – usually at the cost of the ordinary traveler. It was as if he inhabited a different world where rules, so binding on us, were his to obey. For people like me, he was just an unavoidable nuisance to put up with.

Already on the verge of surrender, I had almost decided to discontinue the journey, when the *Bakshi* sprang a surprise. It was the first time, during the entire journey that he let us into his motive behind pushing us to our limits. He announced,

"The Emperor will be unveiling the spectacle of the world in a few days' time. He has planned a big fireworks display followed by handsome donations. If you wait for the *jagirdar* to clear the way, you will miss the opportunity to witness the show of a lifetime and also the pieces of gold and silver. Now, it is up to you – I plan to carry on…"

After much debate and intense convincing by the *Bakshi* and William, a few decided to go ahead. I was one of them.

The alternate route that the more intrepid of travelers had found out was a lot more dangerous and presented a new set of difficulties. It was an old, unused road that had but a few broken shelters and ran through the heart of some of the most lawless villages in the Empire. In short, it was a wild gamble that only those with nothing to lose and everything to gain, would be willing to take.

The better part of the next two days was spent in arranging for the new challenges ahead. William and I got busy collecting information from people who had traveled that way – the rough direction to take, the shelters to expect and specific regions to avoid. The *Bakshi*, on the other hand, went to the market looking for more armed guards and provisions to help us subsist along the way.

Finally, on the day marked for the travel, after seeking blessings at the shrine of Nizamuddin, we marched ahead – a slightly depleted troop of desperate travelers.

This phase of our journey was made under the shadow of the imminence of personal harm. We moved in a compact group by day and huddled together at night, constantly looking out for signs of trouble.

Before long, we had crossed Mehrauli, on the outer reaches of Dilli, and proceeded in a south-westerly loop towards Ajmer. After traveling for a while in that direction, we broke off from the Ajmer road at the village of Gurgawa and arched back, in a counter-clockwise fashion, towards Sohna. Our intent was to circumvent the blockade and join the *Badshahi Sadak* beyond Palwal.

The scenery, this time round, was far from inviting. The velvety green that we had been encountering till now was replaced by miles of dusty, barren land. In place of mulberry and acacia trees, all we could see were a few thorny shrubs and jagged pieces of rock. The sun blazed with fury, water was sparse, rain sparser, and the Aravallis in the horizon seemed to mock every ounce of sweat that we were expending. We were on the fringes of the desert and yet every pore in our bodies begged for relief.

After passing through great swathes of scorched territory, we chanced upon a small, nondescript village where an ancient ritual of brutal oppression was being enacted under the full glare of the mid-day sun.

⌒

A row of modest, thatched-roof huts led us to a large clearing area at the centre of the village. There, around a huge peepal tree, was a disorganised semi-circle of animated villagers. A charpoy was laid out at the base of the tree, on which were seated a few grumpy, men. They were a group of five, each clad in a spotlessly white kurta-pyjama, a gigantic turban and a half-sleeved jacket. The one at the centre, obviously the eldest and the most important, was smoking a hookah. It was the panchayat in session – a motley collection of village elders that was the executive cum legislative cum judiciary of the rudimentary administration. It was evident that here, in this village, the panchayat's was the only and the final word.

The object of so much hysteria was a woman at the far end of the gathering. She was of medium height with a beautiful, dusky complexion and had long, knee-length hair that fell across her bent head. She was standing unmoved, as if oblivious to the surroundings. It was only once in a while, after an especially nasty insult hurled by the panchayat, that she would look up, speak a few words in her defence, get abused even more and relapse into that passive state. In those brief moments, her eyes shone with a brilliance that laid bare the feistiness within.

She was the daughter-in-law of the sarpanch. Her crime was that she had married his son against his wishes. Insubordination was her sin and incest was what she was accused of.

The woman and her husband came from the same *gotra*, a fantastic and seemingly timeless concept of lineage. According to legend, the entire world could be divided into a handful of lineages known as *gotras*. The progenitors of these lineages were purported to be sages of extraordinary wisdom. Thus, each lineage could trace its history back, through hundreds of generations, to the misty nascence of human thought and philosophy. Against such a rich tradition of culture and mythology, it was but natural for everyone to believe that a marriage between two from the same *gotra* was essentially a marriage between siblings and, thus, technically an incest. It was an unpardonable act that did not have any place in society.

I found the idea quite intriguing. On the one hand, its simplicity and personification enabled an easy transfer of the story of origin from generation to generation without the presence of documented family trees that would have been impossible to preserve given an ancient and widely dispersed civilization that has seen many a disruption – natural or manmade. On the other had, however, the logic of the story itself, seemed shaky.

I was interrupted in my thoughts by the booming voice of the sarpanch. He barked –

"Does anyone have any objections?"

It was then that William raised his hand and started in a questioning tone. He said, "You are saying that marrying within a *gotra* is like marrying one's own brother. It is a crime that no one here has ever committed. You further invoke the science in the *shastras* and claim that marrying within a *gotra* stunts the gene pool and threatens the very survival of your clan. I have only one question to ask. If you say that intra-clan marriage is unheard of, then for the last hundreds of generations, men here have always married women from other clans. If that is true, then aren't the genes of this woman and her husband diffused enough for them to actually belong to the same clan? By that logic then, are they doing anything in contravention of either scripture or science?"

"Who are you to comment on the wisdom of our sages? In fact, what you are saying is wholly illogical because the moment a woman marries into our clan she relieves her father's lineage and assumes ours. There is no doubt that this sinner has committed a grave sin and should be punished." – thundered the sarpanch.

The punishment was primeval, symbolic and intimidating.

The panchayat pronounced a retribution that was meant to act as deterrence for the future. It was decided that the woman had shamed the honour of the clan and thus needed to be shamed in return. Each of the five *panches* would force himself on her and once tamed, her face blackened, she would be shunned by the village. Incidentally, her husband just got away with a ritual purification and a promise of handsome donations to the priests.

Her fate sealed, the woman was like a block of stone. She looked at all the people she knew, some of whom she adored and respected and others whom she loved. None came to her rescue as she was defiled again and again. She went deep within a shell as vulgar taunts accompanied the fruition of an age-old act of vengeance. They might soil her body, they might blacken her face, but God knew she had not done anything wrong. With prying eyes lustfully invading her privacy, she just closed hers and prayed for the torture to get over.

"Hey Vasudev!", she sobbed, "You are my savior, you are my honour. Please relieve me from this misery and condemn the perpetrators of faith to hell!"

While the other villagers stood and watched, we were no better. After the initial bravado by William, we had all gone mute. The gross injustice was evident to us but, even then, we did nothing. We were quite a few in number with similar feelings, some armed guards of the caravan among them, and yet we too made accomplices of ourselves by hollow sympathy for the woman and her plight. When her painful moans became too much to bear, we just looked the other way and carried on.

"It's not my battle to fight – why does the Emperor not do something about it!", I thought. "Besides, I have my journey to finish!"

It was only when we had put some distance between us and the village and the din had subsided, that I got to think. I was ashamed at my impotence but I also wondered about the vindictiveness with which the tradition was enforced.

Could all of mankind really have descended from those different progenitors, as claimed? Who gave rise to those progenitors? Could the purity of genes within a lineage, be preserved through 3000 years of existence? What was the rationale behind the concept of lineage? Was it, in the ancient times, just a construct to denote allegiance to a particular sage and group? Was the prohibition of same *gotra* marriage a tactic to win more followers into this group? Or, nobler still, was it a clever ploy for people to maintain contact with the outside world, as people from the same *gotra* often tended to live in the same village?

Whatever the real cause was, it must have become irrelevant and obsolete after centuries. What started off as a novel and noble idea had, over the years, hardened into a fanaticism of epic proportions. The common sense that might have accompanied its formulation was instead replaced by a militant faithfulness to the idea without much thought about the spirit. Taken off context and off-limits to any question on its legitimacy, the original idea then became a useful tool for wicked persons to realize their mischievous ends.

The woman in question was no ordinary one. Since childhood she had had a fiery, rebellious temperament. She had always questioned customs and traditions that rendered women unequal beings. She had gone around spreading her new-fangled ideas and questioned even the legitimacy of the panchayat to issue judgments on matters such as these. She had encouraged other women in the village to speak out against injustice and ill-treatment. She had gone as far as choosing her own husband. Her marrying the sarpanch's son, against his wishes, took the revolution to the very door of the panchayat. Much more than threatening the survival of the clan, her rash action had threatened the autocratic way of life that the *panch* was accustomed to. If he could not quell insubordination at home and that too from a woman, what could prevent the other villagers from disobeying him? She had to be shown her place – she stood no chance.

With a sigh, I trudged on. Embarrassment gave way to indignation, indignation to peevishness and peevishness, finally, to apathy. I had seen enough and now I just wanted to reach Agra as soon as possible.

We merged back with the *Badshahi Sadak* up from Palwal, rested for a while at Hodal, crossed Akbarpur and Mathura and moved on. The disturbing events had cast a gloom over the entire group and we covered most of the distance in silence. As we neared Agra, however, the atmosphere outside helped to lighten the mood within.

The closer we came to our destination, the more festive the air got. Colourful banners and streamers fluttered from the trees and rows of shops selling sweets and other delicacies lined the road. The human traffic, too, increased considerably with a steady stream of visitors from neighbouring villages and elsewhere, all bound towards the first city of the Empire. There was visible excitement among them and they chatted in animated voices. With unnerving frequency, the Emperor himself popped up in the form of larger than life cut-outs welcoming the peoples of the world and promising them a spectacle of the likes they had never heard or seen. The *Bakshi* was right, after all.

The festivities reached an almost feverish pitch near Sikandra, at the door of the capital. Trumpeters, drummers, magicians and acrobats jostled with the shops providing entertainment to the passers by. On the road, the crowd itself had grown thick making progress agonizingly slow. Cattle, camels, horses and other animals competed for space with the ever increasing mass of humanity. It reminded me of the great *melas* back home. I was at once happy and pensive.

Elbowing through the crowd, my eyes fell on small, black mounds carelessly dumped on the sides of the road. Curious, I asked one of the *mithai-wallahas,*

"*Bhai,* what are those?"

"Black marble!", he shot back impatiently.

Intrigued, I went and brushed my hand on one of the mounds. Almost immediately, the black paint came off to reveal a spotlessly white slab of marble beneath. Clueless and very curious by now, I decided to investigate it further. The painted blocks of marble, it turned out, was to appease the king of the central hills, Raja Bundel Singh.

A lesser Rajput by birth, the Raja fashioned himself as a messiah of the downtrodden. As a young usurper, he had sought legitimacy through a strident criticism of those dynasties which birth and tradition accorded a higher status than his. He had repeatedly pointed out their injustices and harangued his subjects to unite under his banner and help him dominate the erstwhile enemies. This, they had done willingly, joining him en masse – which, in turn, had further enhanced the *Raja's* standing leading to the stamp of imperial recognition. For, partly in order to maintain his suzerainty in the hills and partly due to the usefulness of the Raja as a counterpoise, the Emperor had gladly embraced him as a strategic ally. Unfortunately, while the Raja's lot improved dramatically, those of his subjects languished as always.

That was a while ago.

By the time the Emperor got engrossed in his dream project, a lot had changed. Political equations were different and the Raja not so essential in the Emperor's scheme of things. A ravenous hunger for marble, artisans to chip them and implements to chip them with, made him turn his attention away from the Raja and look towards the quarries and factories in the west. Each passing day, as favours diminished, the Raja sulked and peeved and whined. Till one fine day, a brilliant idea struck him. "Surely, that must be the only way to get back in business!" he thought.

The project that had so devoured the Emperor was a monument of astonishing grandness. Aside from men and money, he had needed enormous quantities of marble to wrap it up in splendor. Fortuitously for the Raja, the marble was white in colour. And that gave him a whiff of opportunity.

For the last few months, as the construction had proceeded to its climax, the Raja had gotten busy attacking what the monument stood for. He had sent self-righteous missives to the Emperor, stating –

"The marble, by virtue of its colour, is not representative of my people. I would urge you to reconstruct it with black marble…"

When the Emperor had chosen to ignore him, he had simply upped the ante. In his subsequent messages, he became more combative, claiming –

"We have, for long, suffered discrimination at the hands of others. By continuing to do so, I will let my people down. Thus, I request you to demolish and rebuild the monument with black marble, or build an identical one in black. In case you fail to do so, my people will be forced to agitation and, as you know, I could scarcely do anything against my people's will…"

The Raja was correct about his assessment.

For, the Emperor, busy as he was, did not want a war at this most crucial juncture in his life. As the Raja might have guessed, the Emperor did two things. During day, he had a few blocks of marble hastily painted in black and made a great show of transporting them to a designated place east of the *Yamuna*. Under the cover of night, and not so conspicuously, he slipped in a *peshkash*, a royal gift comprising of elephants and gold to the eager Raja. Miraculously, after months of intensity the agitation simply fizzled out and died a natural death. The Raja pacified, the Emperor got back to his project once more.

Meanwhile, if the monsoons had been on time that year, it would have washed away the superficial paint and, with it, all the sins that it represented. Nature, as one might be tempted to think, often mixes sarcasm and irony in going about her ways.

⌒

By now, unknown to myself, I had been pushed and shoved around to the front of the crowd. We took a sharp turn and there, right before our eyes, stood the grandest of grand monuments, the spectacle of the world, the symbol of imperial prestige, the pride of the Empire, the palace of palaces – The Palace of The Crown!

It was a truly remarkable sight, the stuff that dreams are made of! On a vast, level expanse of land stood the grand monument, towering over and looking down on everything in the vicinity. Awestruck, as we approached it through a majestic arched gateway, the brilliant symmetry was immediately apparent. For, as viewed through the middle of the arch, half of the monument, its gardens and, in fact, the entire surroundings seemed an exact mirror image of the other.

Crossing the gate, we entered the gardens of heaven. A thick carpet of green, as luxuriant as a Persian rug, was lavishly spread out before us. Streams of water, dotted with man-made fountains, came in from the four sides culminating into a slightly raised platform in the middle. From there, one could sit and marvel at the beauty of the palace in front.

The palace itself was the cynosure of thousands of stupefied, wonderstruck eyes. Wrapped in a spotlessly white blanket of marble, it smirked at the brilliance of the mid-day sun. Delicately carved with intricate designs, studded with emeralds and rubies and ornamented with elaborate filigrees, it trumpeted the arrogance of its existence and that of its creator. For, today, the sun, despite all its dazzle, was but a pale shadow of the magnificence in front of our eyes – it burnt with a zealous, infuriated and ultimately fruitless envy. Time, too, had stilled bowing in deference to this timeless grandeur.

Going through the building, caressing its smooth walls and taking in the fragrance of the beautiful gardens, I could not help but be moved by the poetry. I looked at the beauty on offer and thought about the squalor back home and said to myself –

"If there is paradise on earth, it is this, it is this, it is this…"

The Emperor was to arrive any moment and, knees bent, heads bowed we waited as the royal master of ceremonies started to the accompaniment of drums and trumpets –

"Beware! Here, on this blessed piece of land, descends His Exalted Highness, The Magnificent One, The King of Kings, The Liberator of Men, The Protector of Women, The Dispenser of Justice, The Benefactor of Friends, The Vanquisher of Enemies…."

He stopped mid-sentence. He had run out of adjectives.

Regaining composure, he carried on while followed by a long retinue of relatives and courtiers, the Emperor shuffled in, an unsure, old man. He climbed the podium while the gathering arranged itself according to royal protocol. In the front were the Emperor with his favourite sons and daughters and at the back were the courtiers in decreasing order of importance – their backs humped from all the groveling at court.

To the Emperor's left was Sufi, the scholar, his most favourite son and the heir apparent. To his right was Baaz, the hawk, the most likely successor.

Since childhood, Sufi had been groomed to take over the reins after the Emperor. He had always stayed by the Emperor's side, leaving him awestruck by the depth of his knowledge and the liberalism of his views. He had gained steady prestige in the eyes of the Emperor, the latter having gone so far as to anoint him publicly as the next in line to rule Hindustan.

On the other hand, while Sufi had drowned himself in philosophy and mysticism, Baaz had been busy in warfare, an able general, marshalling his troops to victory. However, irrespective of his achievements on the field, Sufi's off it had always been dearer to the Emperor. Frustrated at his state and unable to win favour, he had looked elsewhere. Where Sufi had gained by an enthusiastic championing of inter-faith harmony, Baaz had sought to gather other disgruntled elements and plotted to denounce Sufi as a heretic and a sinner. These disgruntled elements, incidentally, were holy men long shunted out of their once pre-eminent positions in politics. That had definitely angered them but, what pinched more, was the marked decrease in royal grants that accompanied it. Thus, in making fanaticism and austerity as his planks, Baaz had found zealous conspirators in his cunning plot to overthrow the Emperor and his chosen son.

I looked at the royal family and could not help but get alarmed by the precariousness of the Empire. By embarking on the path of wanton extravagance, the Emperor was on the road to financial and political ruin. Something told me that succession would be a bloody affair where Baaz's cunningness would prevail over Sufi's inexperience. He would come to power by the sword of faith and be very eager to display his pious credentials. This would lead him to try and impose his piety and his orthodoxy on his subjects – something quite dangerous for the ruler of a land, so diverse, to do. Citing austerity, he would denounce his father's faithless extravagance and impose discriminatory taxes that would alienate a large section of the people. The taxes would not contribute much to his treasury, but would add a significant amount to his woes. For, when the Empire would be threatened by insurgencies in its outer reaches, he would not find help and support within. Further, his measures of austerity would ring hollow as he would saddle his treasury in a misguided and costly war to the south. His generalship and cunning would win him the Deccan, but would make the Empire a spent force ripe for disintegration by a flood of divisive forces unleashed by his myopic policies. In time, Baaz would be a repugnant vulture hovering over the carrion of an empire built so assiduously by his ancestors.

An arrogant Emperor, a myopic prince and William's vitality against this backdrop – it was a morbid thought, but one not entirely without introspection. For, it was not always this bad. Under *The Great Man*, the present and the future were remarkably rosier. Where the Emperor had been born into wealth and splendour, The Great Man had to build his empire brick by brick. A towering leader of men as inspiring during peacetime as in war, he neither had the time for vanity, nor for insularity. For a monarch with the supreme lordship of one of the largest empires of the world, he was unusually kind and considerate. He had tried to bridge the religious divide, maybe from a quest for the metaphysical or from a realization of the benefits of inclusiveness. His zeal for securing peace and scouting for talent sans prejudice had ushered in a glorious era of prosperity. Imbibing the best from every quarter, he had made the growing, selling, procurement and taxation of crops smoother and more equitable. Administration was better managed and a lot more efficient. He had also taken an active interest in the science of warfare, securing the best for his troops. Above all, he was able to unify the different warring factions of this great and diverse land into a strong, centralized authority. In short, he created the entity of Hindustan – a feat unmatched in recent memory.

From then to now was a downward trend, but the future portended worse.

The Emperor, meanwhile, shifted uneasily on the dais. In his roving eyes there was an inquiring look that wanted to know how history would judge him. I looked at the Emperor and his colossus of arrogance and thought that all we were fighting about were the means of producing the chisels to cut the marble, the colour of the monument itself and the religious sanctity that it had. In the process, we seemed to be missing one simple point that, for every rupee that the Emperor spent stoking his vanity, he threw a paisa towards us and, after greasing the palms of corrupt officials, precious little was left.

It was a sorry state of affairs, but how long could it continue?

Just then, as if reading my thoughts, William whispered in my ear,

"What you need is a rule of the people, for the people and by the people!"

The idea was novel, but I was far from convinced. I knew that history was a great teacher but we are not necessarily sincere students. I knew that the real challenge was to elevate the interests of the country beyond those of the self. Would a mere change of the rule or the ruler be able to achieve that? As long as we the people keep citing helplessness, won't there always be an arrogant ruler with his hawkish opponent and pliant officials coupled with the destructive energies of the rabble rouser and the opportunist? Will mere cynicism ever help us in building the country that we all long for?

Ultimately, the leaders we get are the leaders we deserve and to cleanse politics, we have to first redeem ourselves. As in the words of the prophet, we need to 'be the change that we wish to see in the world'.

I was submerged deep in my thoughts when someone threw a slipper at the Emperor. He ducked. I woke up. There was Sundar with his deadpan expression –

"Bugger! Don't you have an interview to attend!"

9
THE BIN

The interview was a mildly ambivalent affair.

I was ushered into a room where a lady sat in a stiff, upright posture inspecting a sheaf of papers lying on the table. She had a curious look of incomprehension that could put you at ease only if it were not for her looks. For, she was stunningly gorgeous!

She had neatly combed, straight, shoulder-length hair that curled ever so slightly at the edges. A few strands fell carelessly over the pencil thin eyebrows that drew attention to a pair of big, shapely eyes generously layered with kohl. They were in a state of lively excitement, roving from one corner to the other. Her lips, pouting and a bright crimson, held a perpetually opaque smile. Attired in a body hugging grey suit over a white blouse, she was made to lead you astray. But, it was that constant smile that wore you down. For, hidden behind its opacity, it was impossible to read her mind. There were all the signs, though, of it being a sieve that carefully held on to all that was coarse and gave a pass to anything that was nuanced.

With a burst of unnatural energy, she leaned forward and said –

"Hi! Good Morning!"

"Thanks, Good Morning to you too!" – I replied with an equal amount of positive energy. I wanted her to feel that it was the best morning in my life.

She went on –

"We are in the business of consulting. Our value proposition is our deep understanding of the customer which enables us to offer an array of products and services that are uniquely tailored to her needs. With our suite of industry-benchmark offerings, we strive to touch the customer in various ways and make her life more meaningful…"

In her overt reliance on generics, it was evident that she was clueless. I finally relaxed and switched off as she kept peppering me with jargon.

All of a sudden, she stopped and asked –

"How do you think VM has prepared you for this job?"

It was a tricky one and I paused a while before answering.

"I came to VM as an impressionable young man who knew little about the world outside. The last few years have been a great experience where I have learned to adapt and adopt the best from the different, often contrarian ways of thinking. I have benefited a lot from this contact, given that I have often had to use my own judgment, without depending on others. It has made me independent in thoughts and actions. Last, but not the least, the feeling of exclusivity that a place like VM spawns has given rise to a massive ego. I have been tempted to think that 'if he can do it, I can do it better' or, commonly still 'if he drives a sedan, I need an SUV'...."

I noticed that the lady was on the verge of giving up on me. Her porous mind, on the lookout for keywords, was not paying much attention to the details. Time for course correction, I thought –

"Essentially, my stint at VM has made me a team-player and a go-getter not afraid to take ownership!"

The checklist was ticked. I got the job!

We were a company that really cared a lot for the customer. And, we did touch and enrich her with our services.

To cut a long story short, we were middlemen that brought the rich and the bored closer to the surgeon's scalpel and aided in boosting their sagging morale. True, we also had a nice, uplifting package that provided guided tours but, for the most, we worked with sand.

We called ourselves The Buxom Incorporated. Or, in short, The Bin!

The purpose and objective of the company were very eloquently put before us during induction, the day of initiation into the new order. In approximation of the 'Maslow needs', leaders came and talked about why we existed followed by managers who elaborated on what we did for existence while, at the fag end, came HR and payroll with their more personal insights on how we existed. It was no surprise that as much as the leaders harped on future possibilities, the managers were more concerned with the operational details of the present while the HR was keen on past accomplishments. It was a curious mixture having ample scope for interpretation. For, at the end of it all, the believers among us felt that there was but an imperceptible gap between what we were and what we should be – in any case, if there were any gap, they were more than willing to bridge it. The skeptics, on the other hand, felt that the gap was too wide to bridge, especially given the incentives on offer.

After all the talking, the talkers gave way to the doers, the lowly executives who did the dirty work. One of them, Maddy, was to be my buddy. The proverbial deadweight to enthusiasm, he was not a buddy you wanted to have in your very first job.

Maddy came from a family that had made its mark manufacturing rubber. Fired by the burning passion to 'put a condom in the hand of every man', his dad had worked day and night building a business empire from naught. The liberal appetite for sex and the newly liberalized economy had generally worked in his favour, but there could be no doubt about his commitment to the cause. It was, thus, a rude shock when his own son had been vocally dismissive of all that he had perspired for. Over time, the gulf between dad and son had grown with the former becoming increasingly petulant about the latter's lack of interest in business. He had chided his son's insincerity and often been nastier. Maddy, the condom scion and butt of many a joke at school, had been stung most by a pregnant abuse that his dad had once hurled at him. In a fit of exasperation, the dad had sighed – "Condoms don't work! I rue the day you were born!"

That had been the nail in the coffin and Maddy, as if to cock a snook at his father, had joined the corporate world. It was a big setback to the father as well, but pride had always come in the way of rapprochement. Instead, he buried himself in his work while his son languished in corporate alleyways, his waywardness secretly subsidized by the mother. Today, the father, old and limp, still produced enough condoms in a year to buy The Bin several times over. Incidentally, it also gave Maddy, his son, the carte blanche to screw around.

Partly due to this and partly due to his inherent nature, Maddy was the only one who stood erect in the face of tremendous intimidation by Fixit.

Fixit, our manager, was a testosterone of a man. Dripping with aggression, he prided himself on his ability to fix things. Targets, to him, were meant to be exceeded and opposition, if any, to be broken. With a mug full of adrenaline, he would let himself loose every morning fixing and sorting issues in his way. His thumping boots and exaggerated swagger would be a wake up call for us to hunch in front of our computers, his presence betrayed by the unmistakable trail of destroyed egos that he would leave behind. Stingy with praise and public with criticism, he was every inch a man who had been posed serious questions about his manhood, the night before.

Fixit's preferred style of management was blitzkrieg. To colleagues, both above and below, he would throw an unsettling flood of initiatives, which would touch all of us in a variety of uncertain ways. Some of them would be tactical and some strategic, with a few decoys slipped into their midst. The decoys would be unfortunate orphans left alone to perish by themselves – their misery, useful alibis in Fixit's campaign. For, he would use their abject failures to shore up the modest outcomes of the other few. Discerning adversaries would, at times, question the significance of his successes only to be caught off-guard and cornered in a classic pincer move. In short, by continuous and often unwanted tinkering with people, processes and policies he would gain a lot of repute as the best in change management.

Fixit's rise in the organization had been meteoric, an unfortunate casualty of which had been the severe shortage of lunch partners. To his dismay, the higher he grew the lonelier he became at lunchtime – an alarming situation, for he began using us to fill this void. These days, he would often drop in at our table, unannounced and uninvited on his weekly bout of socializing. He wanted to be one of us, he would say, and crack lame jokes to boot. Faced with this predicament, we would be forced to smile but it was SLal who would laugh the loudest.

The supine Shivendu Lal was a perfect foil to Fixit. He too was blessed with the irresistible urge of pressing forward but, in his case, the modus operandi was markedly different. For, his aggression was much subtler. With a manic obsession to suck his way up the corporate ladder, he had a natural flair for stakeholder management. Maybe it was his favourite sitcom or maybe because he sucked in a thick Scottish accent, we referred to him as Sir LicksALot, or SLal. He was Fixit's pet in his inexorable march towards success.

It was a no-brainer that Fixits and SLals always thrived in pairs.

And then there was Big Daddy, the master of long-winded sentences. A bookish man, the burden of leadership, it seemed, had been thrust upon him. Indecisiveness was his forte, being a terminal bore his destiny. Of him, it should suffice to say that if he wanted to meet you in the afternoon it was a sin to have rice at lunch.

We were an unlikely bunch with disparate job responsibilities. I designed colourful brochures for SLal to solicit clients with, while Maddy handled irate customers angered by our inability to keep the promises we made. We all loved our jobs. I liked the opportunity it gave me to experiment with phallic symbols, SLal loved the rewards it gave him and Maddy got a major masochistic kick out of it. For, at home with customers mothering him, he loved to stonewall them with his disconcertingly stoic response –

"I understand the pain it has caused you Ma'am, but I can't do much about it!"

Our official designations hinted at a sense of continuity that we never had and gave us a degree of importance that we never possessed. No one ever sought our advice, but we still called ourselves 'Consultants'. I was the 'Pre-sales Consultant', SLal the 'During-sales Consultant' while Maddy was the 'After-sales Consultant'. The titles had always been enigmatic to me and one day, with the printer not working and all three of us standing in an assembly line churning out hand sketched brochures by the dozen, I was stung by self-doubt. Turning towards SLal, I asked sheepishly –

"What is a 'Consultant'?"

Casting stealthy glances, SLal replied, "Depends – who is asking?"

Maddy, however, was characteristically direct. With a dismissive air, he said matter-of-factly –

"If what a 'Consultant' does is consulting, then I am an Insultant!"

That rested the matter, and we had a hearty laugh with even the diplomatic SLal yielding to a brief moment of indiscretion.

Our typical day at work was long hours spent slouching in front of the computer interrupted by a healthy dose of *chai* sessions. While at our desks we agonized over toplines and bottomlines, *chai* tended to be about necklines and hemlines. Not all of it was carnal though, there was a fair bit of bitching involved as well. In a sense, these were like safety valves that allowed for a harmless release of pent up frustrations. And, ultimately, that was what held us together as a team.

Apart from computers and cups, the other big occupation was meetings. Unlike Fixit, I usually accepted every meeting invite that came my way, frequently turning up in rooms unsure of whether I was needed or wanted. Fixit, on the other hand, did not accept any invite that came to him often leaving us to place bets on his turning up. I think the unexpectedness gave him a wicked sense of power and control over us.

Of all the meetings that nibbled away at our time, none were as unwieldy as the brainstorming sessions. Big Daddy was a great advocate of brainstorming and liable to convene one at the slightest pretext. Unfortunately, though a great advocate, he was a rather incapable practitioner. His meetings would usually start with his visions of the future and the potential that we supposedly locked within us. It would be a long, meandering speech full of motivational balderdash that would have me squirm in agony. Fighting a losing battle against my drooping eyelids and the chettinad curry in a wild somersault inside my belly, I would pine for a private corner to cut out a long, lone fart of my own. That would be hard to come by, especially as Big Daddy next threw the floor open to us. Upset by the torture and somewhat buoyed by the lecture, we would run amok with our ideas suggesting, for instance, a ban on padded bras to brighten our prospects. In his conduct of these discussions, Big Daddy would be like an incompetent shepherd trying to guide his flock home. And, in the absence of Fixit to bark us back in line, it would be a miserable effort.

Brainstorming meetings aside, Fixit would be conspicuous by his absence in an idea generation meeting of any kind. Ideas, to him, came in the way of execution. He always knew what to do and all he ever needed were men that did what he wanted.

⌒

In a spate of nervous energy, our new year would begin from where we left the previous one. There would be a host of things to take care of – old objectives to be visited, new ones to be formed, appraisals to be done and career plans to be discussed. It was that time of the year when the past and future would vie for space while the present quietly faded out of contention. Not that the present would worry much – for, once the dust had settled, it was she who would again reign supreme for the better part of a year. And then, when her time came she would hang like a Damocles' sword, while all the lessons from the past and the careful planning for the future would be mothballed. With unmindful consistency we would, in our tactical battles with the present, tend to put away the war over the future.

It was, thus, not surprising that one day after a typical chastisement from Fixit, I came to know that Big Daddy had been pulled up by the Board.

Years ago, The Bin was a novel proposition in a largely virgin local market. Back then, cosmetic surgery was still in its infancy and our services were readily lapped up by customers at home. Additionally, by providing quality services at economical prices, we made ourselves attractive in the global market as well. To woo the foreigners further, some bright chap augmented the appeal with a tourism package that stressed on spirituality and karmic crap. We sold the concept aggressively reminding customers of our holistic experience that lifted the mind, alongwith the body. In short, the concept was a hit and we returned stellar performances over several quarters..

However, the nature of the business was such that it was hardly, if at all, immune to competition. Within a few years, there were copycats mushrooming, each of which promised larger outcomes and more intense spirituality at much lower prices. Consequently, growth flattened making the Board impatient. In time, the rapid expansion of the past began to haunt our future. On the one hand it created a success story that became increasingly difficult to emulate and, on the other, the relentless focus on sales usually came at the cost of after-sales support leading to a bunch of very dissatisfied customers.

Thus, in the face of intense pressure from both sides, *Big Daddy* was served an ultimatum to turn around the business or perish with it. Slow to act and theoretical in approach, he was simply not the man for the job.

His first reaction was to bury himself in books. The books told him that he could win if he were able to sniff out the five habits that make people successful and the four pitfalls that a chief should guard against. He also came to know what motivates employees and how, with the right amount of belief, every challenge could be made into an opportunity. In short, he was given a set of tools that he could mix and match for instant results as in a fast-food restaurant.

Loaded and convinced, he wanted to wage a war on symbolism. It was his unshakeable belief that symbols often determined how people worked and having the right symbols was a sure recipe for success. He reasoned that the organizational culture had got trapped in the quagmire of the past, from which it needed an urgent reclamation. And, the biggest obstacle, it appeared, was our logo.

Our company logo, designed when we were smaller and our future brighter, was a narrow, multi-coloured triangle that stood for what the employees loved to do. The triangle was hemmed in by sharp edges, the corners of which had the following in a comic font – *EAT WORK PLAY!* It evoked a sense of free spirit that was somewhat anachronistic given that these days we worked more and played a lot less.

Clearly, Big Daddy wanted fresh ideas and what better than a brainstorming session!

He called all of us into a big room and began with an emotional and slightly tense opening act. Appealing to our better senses he exhorted, thus –

"Guys, as you all know we are in a very difficult position today.

There are a lot of challenges both within and outside the business that we have to sort out. While we need to tackle these day to day issues, I think we need to focus more on the big picture. What do we stand for? How do we take ourselves forward? How do we make ourselves believe in a better future? In my opinion, we are too backward-looking – how do we build a culture that is more progressive? I feel that we ought to do something so that we all feel enriched and empowered by the work that we do…"

He could have gone on and on but Fixit, who for once had willed himself to attend a meeting as open-ended as this, cut him short –

"I too think our logo is retro. Why not change it to *EAT WORK PARTY*? And, maybe put the 'work' in a larger font?"

"That's a good idea!" – said a pleased Big Daddy.

"Great idea makes a lot of sense!" – chimed in SLal.

"But, beyond that, we also need to take a fresh look at the symbol and evaluate what it says of us. The current triangle, with all its narrowness, seems to suffer from an acute identity crisis. It seems to me that we are not sure about ourselves, narrow in our outlook and unwilling to accept fresh ideas…"

By now, Maddy was thoroughly disgusted. He said –

"Don't you think we need to talk about a more robust after-sales support? Don't we also need to think about how we differentiate our services better? Otherwise, how is it ever going to work?"

"Let me spank that impertinent brat!" – thought Fixit.

Big Daddy, was much more parental – "I agree that there are these operational details, but I think they would be natural corollaries of a more vibrant culture. If we are able to get the basics right, everything else would follow."

Undaunted, Maddy was blunt –

"That's true. So, if you think that the acuteness of the triangle is the root of all evil, why not change it? In fact, why not make it obtuse? That way, we would appear broader and seem to embrace change with open arms!"

We were all caught off-guard – nobody ever expected Maddy to say something constructive.

"Brilliant!" cried Big Daddy – he could not believe that things were falling into place. Maybe they needed this pep-talk, he thought. Maybe they are all 'Type B' people, he concluded.

The critical part over, remainder of the meeting was spent thrashing out how the new logo would look with precise responsibilities being given to different teams – some had to make a huge cut-out and place it at the entrance while others had to make sure that it became part of the office stationery. Fixit, ill at ease with unstructured problems, finally came into his own – he jotted down responsibilities, allotted definite timelines and put in place a tracking mechanism to monitor progress. He had tasks, he had deadlines and he had a whip – off he went.

Only Maddy remained unmoved by the wave of enthusiasm – his head shaking in disbelief, his eyes barely containing the incredulity.

The new logo was inaugurated with much fanfare. The triangle had turned upside down and ate up a much larger space at the gate. Clearly, things had changed. But, that was just about the only success that Big Daddy could claim.

The symbol changed but the work remained the same. Gradually outplayed by a leaner and meaner competition, we let our customers down even more. In a matter of months, the new symbol had lost its sheen as well. The cut-out team had been less than diligent in its work and the glue applied was inadequate. Letters began to fall off and the huge cut-out eventually morphed into a looming portent of attrition. For, it now said – ***EAT WORK PART***!

10
A BIT OF US

In a matter of seconds, the shapes on the ground hurtled towards me getting bigger and bigger. On the first thud, the voice rang out –

"Ladies and Gentlemen, welcome to Netaji Subhash Chandra Bose International Airport, Kolkata. Please remain seated in your seats till the aircraft has come to a stop and the captain has switched off the 'Fasten Seatbelts' sign…"

It was time to move. I unbuckled and got up banging my head against the overhead cabinet. Averting the look of disgust on the wife's face, I stood in an awkward limbo till the aircraft had actually come to a stop and the captain had switched off the 'Fasten Seatbelts' sign.

Wife and kid in tow, I was visiting Durgapur. It was long in coming. It was the Pujas. I was anxious.

Getting out of the airport, I caught hold of a yellow-cab driver. I asked him –

"*Dada*, can you take us to Durgapur?"

"*Matha kharap* – are you crazy? It is three hours from here!"

"So what? I will pay you fifteen rupees to a kilometer.."

"*Taka-r groom dekhaben na*! Don't show off your money. I have to get to lunch. I don't have time!"

Rebuffed, I went around looking till I finally found one who was willing to go all the way.

Packing our large suitcases at the back, we took the rear seat – one happy and contented family.

Leaving behind the sprawling cacophony of the City of Joy and the dignified tranquility of Dakhineshwar, we crossed the Hooghly and merged with the G.T. Road.

The sun was kind, probably a shade indulgent, and nature was robed in bright green. My young child, who had seldom seen such greenery before, gazed open-eyed at the trees, the flowers and the ponds rushing by. The setting was alien and he had the look of bewilderment that desperately searched for answers.

For, going to Durgapur was like going back in time. It might have been hardly a couple of decades ago, it might have been a mere three hour drive from a bustling metropolis but, it represented a way of life that now seemed so remote as to be scarcely believable. It was a life where kids turning the pages of a dog-eared book were not uncommon, a life where summer vacations meant cricket at dawn and football at dusk, a life where Sunday morning television programmes had an enduring charm, a life where 'rainy-days' lightened up your faces while 'rainy-evenings' made you glum, a life where you planned a train journey months in advance, a life where you looked forward to relatives visiting you, a life where your biggest worry was the next term exam, a life where the postman delivered messages of joy and sorrow and a life where the howling wind or the pouring rain made you romantic.

Above all, it was a life you knew among people you met. It was a place not far from where you lived. It was a time when you still had time.

I turned fondly at the expectant pair of eyes looking at me. And, with a hint of nostalgia, I began –

"India is a vast country. Seventh largest in the world, some of its far-flung areas are separated by as much as six hours of flight. That's about as far as London to Moscow or New York to Texas. When one tries to comprehend India, not only size, but also its bewildering complexity tends to numb the mind....."